FRACTURED

A DETECTIVE MAGGIE FLYNN MYSTERY

By

Lisa Fantino

Wanderlust Women Travel Ltd.

Harrison, New York

Hard Cover First Edition: April 2019
Published by
Wanderlust Women Travel Ltd.
600 Mamaroneck Avenue/Suite 400
Harrison, NY 10528
www.WanderlustWomenTravel.com

Cover design by Lisa Fantino
Author photo by Rochelle Cheever
Cover photos: hooded figure and shattered glass by Dreamstime.com
Cover Copyright © 2019 Lisa Fantino
www.AuthorLisaFantino.com

Hard Cover ISBN-13: 978-0-578-43708-8
Paperback ISBN-13: 978-0-9884969-8-9
eBook ISBN-13: 978-0-9884969-7-2

Acknowledgements

Writers work in solitude creating imaginary characters, engaging in make believe conversations, developing worlds that don't exist. Yet writers need a whole team of *real* people to make their words live and breathe in the land of make believe. I truly appreciate the efforts of Team Fantino for whom I give extra special thanks:

Roslyn Barreaux Brendzel for reading it with an editor's pen; Michael Bank, Esq. for reviewing it with a prosecutor's eye; and dear Betty Lev for reading it out of pure love...for the author and the genre;

Deputy Chief John J. Mueller, Commanding Officer, Yonkers Police Investigative Services Bureau, who patiently answered my many questions about police procedure. Please allow for dramatic license if nothing is as it should be;

For the library crew at the Mount Pleasant Library, especially Vivian, Martha & James for your support and encouragement and reeling me in when the cover design was too wacky and colorful;

Derek Lundquist, for comic relief when drafting the catchy news headlines;

Michael Ferraiuolo at Iron Works Studios for patience, talent and creativity in producing the Fractured book trailer; and

The Daughters of Saint Paul for their love, support and prayers most of all.

Purge my sins and I will be clean;
Wash me and I shall be whiter than snow.

Psalm 51:7

Fractured

Chapter One

May 27th

Sometimes God answers prayers, the goodness emanates from within, but tonight he could feel the evil approaching, the way grey clouds drop off the mountaintops, suffocating the sun in a last gasp. The burning in his collar chafed him raw. The hairs stood on the back of his neck as the darkness slithered into his world. It cut through his inner sanctum like nails on a chalkboard, its entrance decidedly ominous as the ancient wooden door to the Gothic stone church creaked open inside the vast chamber. There was a disturbance in the force of this holy place, but he could not lock it out. No, it was his job to let in. *Welcome, all ye who enter here. Demons be damned.*

Father Richard McNamara waited anxiously, not patiently, as he did most Saturday evenings inside the confessional box. The approaching presence was not the innocence of a child who lied to his mother or the morning-after regret of a teenager who lost her virginity in a drunken stupor. This heavy grey pall clouded the air, shrouding it like the burial cloth over many a coffin in the nearby tombs, all but suffocating his hope to escape the confidence and forgiveness he knew he must extend, even to the devil himself.

Lisa Fantino

She was hooded, cloaked in black, as she entered the little box, taking her place quietly on the kneeler before her, where many other sinners had come to examine their conscience. Her baggy boyfriend jeans and stubby frame squeezed into the close confines of a box where life's sins were laid bare. She inhaled without the exasperation or apprehension of someone about to alter their life and take another's. She blessed herself, knowing, certain that the man behind the curtain could do nothing to change the course of events, could do nothing to alter the course he launched all those years ago.

"Bless me father for I'm about to sin. It's been a lifetime since my last confession." She fidgeted after her evening revelation, one gloved hand firming her stance against the prayer ledge, the other hand in her pocket, fingering the trigger like stroking a set of worry beads. It was automatic. She was empowered now, stronger than she could ever remember being, no thanks to him. It felt good, like the world of opportunity opened its door to her for the first time in more than a decade. "I'm going to kill someone today."

There it was, she said it out loud. Confessed to the man who offered forgiveness for a lifetime of torment. Yet there was no absolution for anyone tonight, especially him. She had no patience for mercy. How do you show compassion as a reward for abandonment? Did he even recognize his role in all of it? He may be the chief confessor, but tonight she was judge and jury and his sentence was imminent.

The false security of the two-by-three-foot space kept her safe, at least for now. She was finally in control. What evil waited beyond the church steps was her own inner demon and she could deal with it, she would deal with it. Yes, soon, very soon.

2

Fractured

The reverend, on the other hand, was dumbstruck. In fifty years behind the curtain, he had never had anyone confess to murder or voice their intent to kill. He felt a change on the horizon but he had no words to deal with the shock. His job was to help heal the person from the wicked within, but how do you console the wicked? Do they not feel the disturbance they create with every word, with every step, with every breath they take?

He felt some shelter from the recent sacrament of Reconciliation tonight. What used to be called Confession and take place in the concealed space of a wooden closet was now more informal, more exposed as if releasing sins into the open minimizes their injurious effect. The dark beliefs and practices of the medieval church were now changed, modified to bring more light into the world, but did they? Congregants could now choose to face their priest, one-on-one, look him in the eye and reconcile all. Tonight, he was glad the old church retained the confessional box for it afforded him some protection as much as it extended anonymity to her, today of all days. That's what they both desired...invisibility.

Once I kill him there's no turning back. She could hear the voice inside her head. It screamed for action, but she sat in silence, as if waiting for the next cue. So, why confess? Why now, after all this time? Her inner compass was off course, badly, blowing toward a whirlpool to oblivion. Maybe the waters of the Lethe could make her forget the images which filled her nightmares, but she was not ready to die, not just yet.

"My child, what troubles you so?" He had to ask, to draw her out even though he wanted to bury her, or at the very least to chase her from these hallowed walls.

What troubles me? You're what troubles me? Her impulse had exploded after hearing his pathetic, hollow concern. He resurrected all that bad blood that had gone between them. She tried to drown out the voices but they grew louder, screaming now. *Him or me? Him or me?* She had put him to rest years ago but he was stirring again. This time it would be different. This time it was not going to be a battle that *he* would win.

"Father, I can't let him win, not again." Her voice, unwavering in its conviction. She told him she was hell bent on revenge but for what he didn't know. And if he did, whom could he tell? No one. The privacy seal of the confessional was sacrosanct, unimpeachable, a holier bond than even the attorney-client privilege. Only God would judge here. At least attorneys could break a confidence to stop a future crime. All he could do now was pray, even when facing death.

"Tell me, my child," he pleaded with her. "Maybe I can help. You came here this evening for consolation. Let's talk."

"I'm all talked out Father," she confessed. "No one listens anyway, not really."

"I'm listening, my child."

"My child? Where were you when I was growing up? When I truly needed consolation? When *he* tormented me?" The bitterness filled her mouth like the aftertaste of bile rising in the stomach.

"Talking, now, is overrated," she continued. The very sound of her words released a lifetime of fears and tears.

"Then we can sit, quietly, and when you're ready for absolution, I am here." *Great*, he thought. *I'm locked in a cubicle with a psycho and I must be patient. God, give me strength.* He prayed…for himself…as much as for her.

The silence of the cavernous church space was broken inside the confessional only by her rustling and his pounding heart which he hoped beyond hope did not reveal itself to this troubled soul.

The pause seemed like an eternity…for both of them. Not another soul was in church this evening. How could the city that never sleeps be in a deep slumber, now, when they each cried out for help? Their silhouettes visible to each other through the metal screen, so close, yet with a raging river of death between them. He couldn't push her and she couldn't hold back, not much longer. The usual calming scent of frankincense was stale, dank, saturated with uncertainty, moribund in its choking threat.

"God, the Father of mercies and forgiveness, through the death and resurrection of his Son, has reconciled the world to Himself," he continued praying, begging God to release her. "He brought us the Holy Spirit to forgive our sins. Go now, my child, say one Holy Rosary, pray for temperance and a still heart."

Temperance, she laughed inside. Moderation could not quell a lifetime of rage and the uncontrollable desire to snuff it out.

"I absolve you of your sins in the name of the Father, the Son and the Holy Spirit," he offered her forgiveness and blessed himself with the sign of the cross. "Go in peace," he directed her, praying she would leave.

Slowly, he heard her stir in the shadows, waiting for the sound of her passage from the confessional and out to the unsuspecting streets. *Be gone, away from this place, leave me in peace.* He implored her in silence and hoped God would release her. The pounding of his heart grew louder in his chest, the echoes of his own past creeping in like the vapor of death through the cracks of the ancient chestnut wood.

Slowly, deliberately she reached into her pocket and raised the tiny pistol with its silencer up to the metal screen. He saw the gleam of the pearly white handle as she raised her hand.

"Our Father who art in heaven, hallowed be thy name," he began to pray again, this time for his own sins, his own soul.

The fire spark from the muzzle closed the curtain on his life which went dark in a flash.

Oh, yes, she was freed, in an instant she was released, and nothing could hold her back.

Only God can forgive me now!

Fractured

Chapter Two

The Gothic spires of the Bronx cathedral stood like sentinels over the crime scene as Detective Third Grade Margaret Flynn pulled up to the curb outside Saint Nicholas of Tolentine Church. Her car, like the other official cars, parked every which way, added chaos to the developing story. Flynn had only had her detective shield for a month. She caught the case because of the Memorial Day weekend and being low man, or woman, on the totem pole.

Her partner, Tommy Martin, was twenty-five years on the job, seasoned enough to know the ropes and secure enough to share that knowledge with his rookie partner. He pulled up right behind her, all too glad to have her take the lead on this since he had downed a few brews at his family holiday barbecue a short time ago.

"Hey kiddo, whatta we got?" He shouted to her as the blaring lights of patrol cars seemed to call more Lookie-Lous to the scene rather than ward them off. This corner of the Bronx was rarely quiet, just steps from Fordham University and within spitting distance of Arthur Avenue's Little Italy neighborhood.

"Hey," Maggie acknowledged his arrival, pad and pen in hand. Cops still jotted handwritten notes, down and dirty, and rarely in digital form.

"Church lady going to clean found the body, a dead priest in the confessional," she said with an uplifted chin in the direction of the young cop taking a statement from the witness.

"I bet her sins pale in comparison," Martin quipped, brushing his messy mop of greying hair from his face. He forgot to tuck his shirt tails into his chinos in his rush to the scene.

She rolled her eyes at his sarcasm as they entered the church, neither one could help but reach for the holy water to bless themselves on this most cursed of nights.

Two officers guarded the confessional, the resting place of Father Richard McNamara, who, by all accounts, was a dedicated clergyman, just weeks from an anticipated retirement.

It was almost pointless for any officer to don shoe covers since the inside of the church, any church, was as contaminated as Grand Central Station at rush hour. Defiled was an understatement.

Maggie peered into the priest's entry door to the confessional chamber which had already been opened by the church lady who discovered him less than an hour earlier. The reverend slumped over himself, like a sack of flour unable to hold itself upright, still sitting in the place where he granted forgiveness to hundreds of others during his long career.

"Tell me what you see," Tommy directed his partner.

Maggie began spewing her impressions certain that Tommy was taking notes behind her. There was barely enough room for Maggie to peek inside this hallowed space with a dead cleric for company.

She snapped on the requisite blue latex gloves and with one gloved hand, she gently lifted McNamara's head to look for an entry wound. His priest collar and purple prayer stole were now dripping scarlet with his own blood. The small hole in the metal screen was evidence that the killer shot straight through the privacy divider, shielding the victim from his judge and jury.

"It's tight in here," she explained her own discomfort to her partner. As a Catholic school survivor, it was difficult enough for her to enter a confessional from the priest's entrance, let alone occupy the space with his cold body. This was not her first dead body on the job but the discomfort still tore at her core. She squirmed in the tight confines. As her own leg brushed the cleric's robe, chills shook her from the inside, like crawling, invisible worms, everywhere and nowhere.

Tommy had gone around to the penitent side of the booth and realized that even at close range the shooter was skilled enough to take aim and take down the priest in one shot. He knew from hours of his misspent youth inside the confessional box that it was difficult to see anything more than the priest's profiled silhouette. The priest often sat back in his seat, making nothing more than the edge of his nose and chin visible to someone begging for absolution.

"Does it look like only one shot in there?" Tommy's question forced her to lift the priest's head again, delicately, taking in all sides before forensics and the medical examiner arrived.

"Yeah, looks like one shot through the right temple but no bullet in sight," she explained her assessment of the scene.

"And no shell casing in here," Tommy announced from the other side of the booth. "This was a clean, vengeful hit." Usually only pros stop to pick up evidence of their dirty deeds. Amateurs barely escape without tripping over their own trail of forensic minutia at a crime scene.

They were puzzled but the facts revealed that while McNamara probably wasn't acquainted with his killer, his killer certainly knew him, or at least his habits. Knew he'd be in the confessional box until eight o'clock on a Saturday night. Knew

9

he'd likely be alone or at least waited outside until that was the case.

"Forensics will have a hard time in here, there's dust and fibers and all sorts of crap on the floor and I'm guessing hundreds of prints from an army of sinners," Tommy said. He was clearly frustrated at the contamination that would make their job that much harder. Most evidence is gathered in the first twenty-four hours after a murder and with a contaminated crime scene, usable clues would be hard to come by.

"Not much else we can do here. Let's go talk to the church lady while the Crime Scene Unit does their thing," Maggie talked through the screen as Tommy directed investigators and photographers to go inside the closet of crime, memorializing Father McNamara's last minutes of life.

Seventy-year-old Blaise Gomez was still shaking more than an hour after calling the cops. Murder and mayhem shattered her world in the place where she expected to be safe. She blathered on, trying to make sense of it as she repeated her story to Maggie and Tommy. They had taken her to the rectory next door where someone had prepared a cup of tea to soothe her nerves but there wasn't enough chamomile to wash away this horror.

Only two priests remained in residence at Tolentine and Father Richard McNamara had been one. Gomez had discovered the body when she entered to clean the church and prepare it for Sunday morning Mass. It was her Saturday night ritual just after confession ended. With broom in hand, she happened upon the body.

"*Ay Dios mio*, he was such a good man. We all loavvvve him," she said, sniffling, into a well-used soggy tissue. "Who would do 'dis?" She repeated over and over, as if the refrain

10

Fractured

from a Gregorian chant, said often enough, would make the outcome more palatable. Yet prayers would not be answered, not tonight.

Chapter Three

The night was taking on an energy of its own, sidewalks dressed with men in wife-beater shirts and women in way too much, or too little, belly-baring spandex all craning their necks for a better view of the evening's ugliness. News vans and the annoying reporters who occupy their insides were arriving en masse like paleolithic cockroaches racing out of corner sewers. The yellow crime scene tape barely caught the rare breeze and did little to hold back the neighborhood curiosity. The air outside stagnant, dead, making it hard for many to breathe so early in the season, others gasping as they learned that a priest had been murdered inside this massive, consecrated house of God.

"Hey, Mags," Tommy pulled her aside, aware of Maggie's friends in the media, "It goes without saying but I'm saying anyway, no talking to the enemy."

"You see, Tommy, it's comments like that make those nice folks with microphones try to jam you up." Maggie's bestie, Mickey Malone at CBN, had let her do more than a handful of nighttime ride-alongs, chasing scanner leads, before she ever entered John Jay College and the Police Academy.

Now, years later, Maggie's a detective and Malone's on network TV, too busy for the likes of local homicide.

"Well, I'm learn-ed in the school of hard knocks and if you want a long career and a shiny gold shield, someday, then mind your Ps and Qs, young lady."

"You sound just like my Dad," Maggie said wistfully, wondering what her Dad would think of her new post in the Bronx Borough Detective Division.

"I'm his spokesman, Detective Third Grade Flynn, remember that," he said. Tommy knew her father when he himself was starting out back on foot patrol. Detective Lieutenant Sean Flynn had a stellar reputation in the Department. Tommy imagined his kid, any kid, son or daughter, would have a difficult time living up to that narrative, both the good and the bad.

Maggie fought her inner demons, the insecurity of a woman in a man's world of investigators, even in the 21st Century. There was an internal bias against the kids of cops moving up in rank, as if the honor was anointed rather than earned. She worked harder than most just to prove to everyone, and to herself, that she deserved it.

The local Precinct Commander invaded her mental, nano lapse of insecurity on the broad expanse of sidewalk outside the church steps. Local cops had managed to force the inquisitive neighbors to DeVoe Park on the opposite corner, allowing investigators access to do their job in and around the church.

"Good evening, detectives. I'm Commander Jones of the 46th." He was authoritative, not condescending or reluctant as locals often are to hand over any crime to detectives outside of their control.

"The Commissioner and brass will meet you back at your H-Q in thirty minutes. They need to be briefed before the eleven o'clock news," Jones passed along the directive.

Lisa Fantino

Not knowing how long their night would be, Tommy took his old Jeep and Maggie headed out in her vintage '65 Mustang, driving the half-hour it would take them in Saturday night traffic to reach Division Headquarters on Simpson Street. By the time they arrived, town cars with darkened windows and more news vans than a NASCAR meet occupied most of the prime parking spots and Maggie was very protective of her prized Pony car. It was her Dad's and she learned more than how to drive inside its creamy white leather seats. Sitting next to her Dad, she learned about life. She learned about living. And she learned about death. She convinced Tommy to give her the last cop spot and then block her in with his Jeep, so no one would dent the prized silver blue beauty. She loved its sleek sportiness which glowed like stardust under the streetlights overhead. Maggie was a lot like that car, brilliant and stylish on the outside but sporty with a throaty core that hadn't yet released its full power.

The one-time Fort Apache precinct, so nicknamed because of its beleaguered past in this fiery Bronx neighborhood, now housed the Bronx Borough Detective Bureau on a pleasant tree-lined street. It was the stage for the first act in what could be a long, hot and deadly summer.

Never having been on a case that called for her attendance at a news conference, Maggie was amazed at the behind-the-scenes prep that went into getting ready for the eleven o'clock news. Department brass, news crews, all lining up, getting their stories straight and their gear hooked up to shoot, simultaneously, for what would likely be a pat response from the Commissioner.

Fractured

Tommy suggested they retreat to their desks upstairs and get out of the way until summoned to appear on camera. Yes, this would be her close-up and she wasn't ready.

Assistant Chief Ernest Bradshaw, the Bureau's Commanding Officer, had called Tommy and Maggie into his office and asked to be briefed. He needed to fill in the Commissioner and they would all stand together, a united front of crimefighters, once the press conference started to roll.

"I'll go out on a limb and say the priest was targeted, Chief." Tommy took the lead on briefing the boss and Maggie demurred. She still needed to learn how this game was played but she was a quick study.

"All signs point to the fact that the killer knew his target and was an experienced shooter. One shot, clean, no casings, no bullets except maybe what's inside the priest, nothing left behind."

"And what was the witness doing there?" Bradshaw knew it wasn't much, but they needed at least two minutes to fill the slotted air time at the top of the hour. The orchestrated timing between scheduled police pressers and city news rooms was a ballet of expectation these days.

"She was the church cleaning lady," Tommy explained. "She routinely went in most Saturday nights to clean after confession and get the place ready for Sunday morning Mass."

Maggie spied the time. Just fifteen minutes to go before the city learned how terror rained down on a Bronx church kicking off one hot summer. The Chief's battered, metal desk fan only stirred the tension in the house and did little to cool the slowly rising temperature.

Downstairs, the news roaches seemed to multiply quickly as Tommy sarcastically whispered to Maggie, "Slow news night, a holiday weekend." This would be the lead that

15

bleeds and the Commissioner was already standing near the podium to run with it.

Ten minutes and counting. Now, Ray Peretti, a spokesman for the New York Archdiocese, joined the growing team at the front of the room. As confident as Maggie was most days, she felt out of her element here, as did Tommy. He hated this part of the job. Let investigators investigate and let the brass babble, since they do it so well.

She watched as one cameraman counted down the top of the hour and cued them with a finger oddly pointed like a gun. The Commissioner recited what little facts were available, while Peretti explained the profound loss of New York's Catholic community. The news roaches shouted randomly stupid questions which they knew wouldn't be answered, especially so early in an ongoing investigation. It was a wrap as the hands on the clock in the lobby hit 11:05, as precise and definite as murder tonight.

Chapter Four

There was something so finite about death, yet something so eternally liberating. It was easier than she thought, the taking of a life for the one who had robbed her of happiness. She had this down. Her hair had been secured in a net under the generic black hoodie, which she conveniently tossed in a restaurant dumpster halfway home. Not a New York soul thought it peculiar, her wearing a hooded sweatshirt in the late spring heat wave. She had worn gloves as well. No trace of her malevolence. Fingerprints, fibers, touch DNA, none of it could lead to her in a scene rife with the indiscretions and sins of hundreds of other miscreants, just like the poor padre.

She had secured Pearl safely in the bedroom. No one would find her. This was their secret space. She knew Pearl well, held her tight at night when the outside world threatened to invade her inner sanctum, caressed every line of her taut body, anticipated her response with each pull and discharge. She took care of all her needs, more reliable than any man in her life. And tonight, it was the ultimate release for both of them. Tonight was just the prelude to the even greater task ahead.

Chapter Five

May 28th

Shock and sadness greeted parishioners who arrived at Tolentine Church for Sunday morning Mass only to see the remnants of yellow crime scene tape blocking entry to the main church. Forced to celebrate Mass at the community center around the corner, many congregants just learning why Father McNamara was not today's celebrant of the liturgy.

Maggie and Tommy went to Mass this morning, much like good cops attending a murder victim's funeral. It was a grim reality that there could be a killer among the devoted.

"You feel that?" Tommy asked as they sat in the last makeshift row of folding chairs, looking cautiously upward.

"Feel what?" Maggie eyed the crowd, from left to right and back again, as if she missed something which was obvious to her more seasoned partner.

"The walls shook when we entered" was his quick retort. Maggie understood at once because Catholic school survivors fell into two groups. There were those who observed every religious holiday with a spiritual fervor, attending Mass and confessing everything. Then there were those they called lapsed Catholics who remembered every word to every prayer, every lyric to every hymn, yet never went to church except for weddings and funerals. Maggie and Tommy had lapsed long ago.

"This is just a community center," Maggie reminded him this wasn't a real church *per se*, not like the grand building next door consecrated with a relic of Saint Nicholas of Tolentine.

"Details, details."

"Yes, that's our job, isn't it?" The rookie detective reminding her new mentor.

They worked the remainder of the holiday weekend dissecting the life of Father Richard McNamara while the medical examiner physically cut him open. That part seemed like overkill when a bullet sprayed his brain matter all over the inside of the confessional. Yet heaven help an investigator missing a minute detail, as if a toxicology report revealing evidence of anti-depressants in his system would alter the obvious cause of death here.

Both detectives attended the autopsy. Normally only one was enough to protect the chain of evidence taken from the body but since this was Maggie's first big homicide, Tommy thought she should get her feet wet, so they went together.

"What's this for?" Maggie asked as Tommy offered her a Vicks inhaler stick just outside the autopsy room.

"Roll some under each nostril so the smell doesn't kill you in there," he answered. He had been to more than his share of victim postmortems in his long career. Maybe cops got used to the slice and dice of it all but the smell triggers memories you can never forget. Some scents were pleasant. This wasn't one of them.

Maggie held her own inside as the priest's organs were dissected and removed one by one. The sound of the saw cutting his skull grated on her initially, but then she found herself fascinated by the hunt. It didn't take long for the medical examiner to retrieve the bullet or the fragments left of it. A nine-millimeter bullet had claimed the life of Father McNamara. It went in but it never came out.

Everything, including the bullet fragments, his clothing, his blood-soaked prayer stole was bagged and tagged and initialed to preserve the chain of evidence, to show the world, and eventually a judge and jury who touched and reviewed any one item at any given point in time. Contaminated or lost evidence was to blame for many guilty men and women going free.

They spent what was left of Sunday dividing the mundane chores between them, Maggie taking McNamara's personal history from Father Michael Flanagan, the other priest who lived in the Tolentine rectory, and Tommy canvassing local area shops and neighbors.

The musty smell of old permeated the air in the rectory's front lounge where Maggie was asked to wait for Father Flanagan in the dimly lit room. He was still speaking with congregants on the sidewalk following a special late day Mass and had to disrobe his vestments before returning to meet with her.

The wait inside a rectory never changed for a Catholic school survivor, the nervous anticipation of a priest's arrival. Despite her thirty years, there was something adolescent-like, like returning to the principal's office, while remaining still in this quiet, nearly silent space. She sat a little straighter, composed her thoughts a little clearer as if she were going to meet with God himself.

Maggie turned toward the door as she heard footsteps in the hall, anticipating the solemnity of the meeting. Bolstered by the side arms of her plush chair, she imagined others before her delivering or receiving bad news in this somber sanctum but nothing like this.

"Detective Flynn, this is certainly a sad day for us here," Flanagan reached out to shake her hand as she rose from the well-worn green velvet cushion.

"Father, I'm sorry for your loss," Maggie expressed her understanding but realized she had little time to empathize with a killer on the loose. "I'm hoping that you can fill me in on Father McNamara, his background, who he was, anyone who might wish him harm."

The silent pause seemed like an eternity until Flanagan spoke.

"Detective, by your last name, can I assume that you're an Irish-Catholic?"

"Irish-Italian Catholic," Maggie clarified proudly with a faint smile, "Catholic school survivor, fourteen years."

"Fourteen?" Flanagan, opened his eyes wider, chin retreating into his collar, looking beyond the usual elementary and high school career.

"Yep, started Catholic college but had to spread my wings, if ya know what I mean." She dipped her head coyly, trying to lighten the moment, even if only for a second.

His instant smirk changed the lines of his face. What had been tense, now relaxed a little. His eyes, the color of cool spring water, now sparkled just a bit having known many other such students in his lifetime.

"How long did you know Father McNamara?" Maggie got right to work.

He explained that having only just arrived at Tolentine a few short months ago, he didn't know McNamara long or well.

"I was sent here to get up to speed on the needs of the parish in anticipation of the Father's retirement in just four months." He told Maggie that despite the size of the parish, the Archdiocese was not certain if they would continue staffing with two priests in residence once McNamara retired, so they were exploring all possibilities, one day at a time.

In its heyday, this parish had been one of the largest in the city and its high school was known as a basketball powerhouse with hundreds of students, star athletes and a cadre of clergy. Vastly different from today's smaller elementary school comprised of immigrant children from lower income families.

"We've been suffering a long time here," Flanagan disclosed. "Father McNamara, at seventy-five, was actually looking forward to retirement. He was tired.

"Priests are asked to retire at seventy-five but may continue working as long as they can fully perform their religious obligations

"Preaching and caring for people can be both rewarding and exhausting," he said, as the weariness of the stark new reality returned to his face, "but rarely, if ever threatening."

"Mac," he caught himself, "Excuse me. We are, after all, still people with nicknames and private lives," vacillating again between relaxed candor and official mission statements.

"He was ordained in 1965, before you were born." She appreciated the levity and realized that was the year her classic car was born.

Maggie's hour-long interview revealed a priest who had spent most of his time in the Bronx and the outer boroughs except for a short stint in St. Louis, Missouri. She thanked Father Flanagan for his time and frankness and assured him they would stay in touch as the investigation progressed.

Fractured

Maggie had to adjust her eyes from the dark inner retreat of the priest's world to the bright reality of the Bronx sun as she exited the rectory onto University Avenue. Murder didn't take a holiday and people in the city hurried about their way to evening barbecues and parties as life went on around this theater of death.

A hurried scan of the busy horizon didn't reveal her partner's location but a quick text found him on the near side of DeVoe Park, going block by block, building by building, searching for security cameras with Tolentine in their viewfinder. The nearest traffic camera was eight blocks away. The closest security camera was at the supermarket across University Avenue, but its view was only as wide as its front door, not broad enough to record the front steps of the church or its side entrance.

Tommy approached her from the corner of the Park, holding out an orange slushie for her. "Thanks," she said, nearly inhaling it, parched from the cotton mouth of talking for an hour and the *schvitz* of the eighty-degree temperatures in May. "It's a miracle you're not two-hundred pounds overweight," she teased him.

"Chasing bad guys keeps my ripped physique in shape." The repartee which had developed between them over a short month together flowed as naturally as brother and sister, husband and wife, mentor and student, Abbott and Costello.

"Let's salvage at least the next few hours from this weekend and join the rest of my family's motley crew for a brew and barbecue."

Chapter Six

"I'm in control," Donovan's scream was more like a bellow, like a bull moose in the woods marking his turf. Its hoarse boom filled the empty kitchen. "She thinks she can outsmart the teacher? Who's she kidding?" He slammed the glass so hard on the black granite counter that it fractured into a thousand pieces, chips and shards falling to the floor like a carpet of cracked ice. His bare, hardened feet unaware of the bloody trail he created wherever he stepped.

"Damn," he said, suddenly realizing he would have to work harder now, cleaning his mess and hers. Erasing any speck of evidence. He was never so sloppy and he resented it now. He'd toss the rubbish later and she'd be none the wiser.

For more than a few decades, he had taken a back seat as she lived her mundane life, in the shadows, never speaking out, never revealing the past. Slivers of her life, their past, filled this dusty one-bedroom apartment decorated with doilies and dollies. *Is she five or fifty-five*? He wondered as he canvassed her domain. He always slithered in, unwelcomed, unwanted, unrecognized in her absence.

His disheveled greying locks hung across his brow like a squirrel's tail as he reached into the back corners of her bedroom closet, digging through the old lady clothes, the dusters and elasticized knit pants which were her daily uniform.

He had his own corner on the left side in the back where he kept a few things that she never noticed. He was looking for his box of mementoes. It was a lifetime of trinkets that defined him.

"There you are," he said as if greeting an old friend. He gently lifted the ceiling's acoustic tile out of its track. It had protected his stash for some fifteen years. Not even his shadow knew it existed. There was no need to rummage through the past until now. Silence had long been the status quo and he was enjoying it. He was getting too old for this shit.

Their relationship had long gone dormant until recently and he had enjoyed the break. Donovan didn't miss her. They led separate lives under one roof and he liked it that way. He would never give a woman, any woman, that much power over his emotions.

Now, she seemed to have nothing but time on her hands, time to analyze all that had gone before them. He knew what she was doing. He would not give her the upper hand, not in their bloody game of cat and mouse. Donovan's head pounded at the task ahead of him.

Slowly he carried his stash to her bed, laying it gently atop the matelassé coverlet of lilacs and hydrangeas. The air was still. The scent of potpourri and cat dander scratched the back of his throat and aggravated his asthma. Not even the stupid cat dared to stir near him. Donovan knew that he was opening Pandora's box and contemplated the rush of that first kill all over again.

His hand moved in the direction of the metal latch on the vintage Scooby-Doo lunchbox. He chuckled, realizing she had been trying to root out evil, his evil, since they were kids. The stale air which emanated from this vault of gruesome souvenirs assaulted his nostrils. Breathing was so hard for him. It smelled like rancid milk and death and attacked the rose petal scent which permeated this tiny home.

Soon, very soon, Donovan would add to his box of collectables. He had randomly visited his killer's cache over the years to admire his handiwork. Little did she know how in control he'd always been.

The metal coffer of death held a friggin' doily, a gold cross, a ruby ring, an honor roll student badge, an actual baby tooth and a baby bracelet with a lock of hair. There was also a baby's pacifier, which he fondled habitually before placing it in his pocket. Some women, weak, immature women, always held onto such infantile keepsakes of youth. It boggled his mind as to their inexplicable reasons.

His conviction to silence their nonsense, however, never wavered. They suffered from an inability to speak up and when they did, it was always in a whisper. They always seemed to be asking permission for something they were entitled to, never asserting a right that was theirs for the taking. He'd put them out of their misery, especially her.

He admired the ruby ring from kill number three, holding it up toward heaven with reverence as if holding a bejeweled, golden chalice. It caught the sunlight through the lace curtains. The glimmer of the blood-red stone mesmerized him briefly. A prism of light to a new life...until he noticed the engraving inside the band, "Love Mom & Dad." *Awe, how sweet, Mom and Dad and their little girl, Ruby.* He found it all so amusing. His life. Their deaths.

There was nothing sweet about his resurrection. She pushed him to it. She'd make him start working again. This time she jumped on his bandwagon, trying to copy him, stealing his thunder and headlines. Beat him at his own game? *Ha! She's never gonna win!*

Fractured

He locked the cache with a snap of the latch and placed it back in its covert den. No one would find what he refused to reveal. His secrets were all that stood between him and a nine by twelve cage to spend his golden years.

The cat, which had been reluctantly watching from the corner of the room, lashed out at him with a piercing cry and a thrashing paw as Donovan slid the closet closed. He kicked at it and missed, tripping over the small area rug now speckled with his blood, quickly escaping attack as he ran from this place and all that he left behind.

Freedom returned as he stepped into the late spring evening. He stretched like the cat that he hated, then cricked his neck and arched his broad shoulders as if gearing up for a game of gladiators.

Donovan thought about where he could prowl for prey. He had to ease his way back into the hunt. He hadn't planned it and acting on the fly had never been part of his M-O. Sloppy kills make for stupid mistakes and no one, not even the cops, ever accused him of being stupid or sloppy.

McLean Avenue was relatively quiet for an early Sunday evening. Despite a five-block swath of Irish pubs and the noise they bring on any given Friday or Saturday night, this was Sunday, a day for families. It was an evening when moms nagged their kids about homework not quite done at eight o'clock and due first thing in the morning. Ahh, yes, families, can't live with 'em, can't kill 'em.

He crossed the border into the Bronx in the three short blocks from her apartment. No need to hunt so close to home unless you want to get caught. He wasn't stupid. Tonight, he was just warming up. He'd spare any woman who caught his eye…at least that was his plan.

27

The number of Irish pubs along this stretch of Katonah Avenue made McLean look like a neighborhood of teetotalers. Even the cops drank here. *Yes, be careful, Donovan, lest you run into anyone she knows.*

It took him awhile to find just the right stool in just the right gin joint. It looked like a watering hole for lonely, middle-aged retirees. Complaints about the weather, the Yankees and bad kids on dark corners carried throughout the room but no chat about family dinners. *Such losers, such lonely, lonely losers,* he thought as he hunted.

Don't make eye contact. Keep to yourself. He mulled his prey and knew better than to chat up anyone at the pub. *Stay in the background. Become part of the woodwork. Take it all in and leave after one drink.* He set his own course for the night's work.

His internal dialogue had him reviewing the skills, the playbook, his game plan which let him kill successfully, repeatedly and undetected, all those years ago. Yet the landscape had changed in fifteen years. Now, lonely-hearts stayed home and surfed the Internet, trolling for companionship in the grey web of life.

Donovan caressed his beer bottle like the lines of a woman's neck. He cautiously eyed the bartender's habits from the darkened shadows of a highboy table along the window. These were the tables meant for loners and losers. The tables meant for folks with nothing to talk about and no one who cared. The tables meant for those suckling on a beer bottle hoping it was something else.

He noticed that when the bartender cleared the bar top of empty bottles, they were tossed, like the bad rubbish they were, haphazardly into a huge blue recycle bin. Good luck with trying to trace sweaty fingerprints in that heap. They'd be long gone come morning, just like him.

28

Fractured

He also knew quite well that no one in a bar would talk to a middle-aged drinker sitting alone in a dark window, so he was secure in his anonymity. There were two kinds of lonely people in bars. Those who wanted to chat up anyone and everyone and those who simply wanted to be left alone. They desired a new dark corner to curl up in rather than the lumpy, hardened discomfort of their living room sofa. Stranger in a strange joint, his image would remain hidden from the crowd of unsuspecting faces.

He left McGinty's Bar realizing he would need to satisfy his predacious appetite in new ways to maintain cover. He was overthinking this as he turned right onto East 238th Street. The blackness of the May evening offered shelter in this residential neighborhood of brick and shingled semi-detached homes. Most houses in Woodlawn stayed in the same family for years until the last generation just shriveled up and died inside its walls or a developer knocked it down to build an even bigger multi-family monster.

Donovan slithered down the concrete pavement, like a panther, not making a sound, making it easy to sneak up on her. He remembered that a twelve-step program met Sunday nights as he came upon the old Presbyterian church on Martha Avenue. He spied her as she put out the trash left by the group before making the short walk home.

Donovan, feeling a little peckish, inhaled the spring air deeply. He could give in, feed his hunger again. He didn't plan on it tonight but what the hell. A little taste wouldn't hurt and he always carried a pair of rubber gloves in his pocket just in case he got the urge.

This poor soul was his perfect muse and he needed practice. She walked along, unassuming, lifting the rusty gate latch in front of her own stoop. Most certainly decent in her helpfulness, virgin-like in her naiveté, feeble in her middle ages.

The shade of darkness covered her house, not a light in a window. He assumed she lived alone, or at least no one else was home, as he creeped up the steps behind her. She made it so easy for him as he pushed his way from the porch and straight through her front door.

She didn't have time to flip the switch in the foyer as her lights went out and would stay that way forever. She went limp in an instant as his gloved hands applied firm pressure over her mouth and nose. He held her in place as what little energy she had sputtered into nothingness. He felt the life leave her body and it reenergized him. He dislodged his hands from around her windpipe, carefully taking the heart-shaped locket draped across her ample décolleté. He felt alive again. Just like riding a bike. You never forget the feeling.

He quietly closed the door behind him. No need to linger. No need for him to admire his work, to get caught. He came, he saw, he conquered. He locked the door on the night and disappeared into the shadows with a new purpose.

Fractured

Chapter Seven

May 30th

The blue flu seemed to grab hold of much of the squad the Tuesday after Memorial Day. Ernest Bradshaw was certain that if he canvassed Long Beach or City Island, he'd find many of his detectives out on their boats rather than returning to work after a long holiday weekend.

"Morning, Chief," Maggie said as she placed the tray of five Dunkin' coffees on her desk. The old laminate top bore the scars of too many coffee cup rings from too many early mornings or late nights before her time. She knew it would likely be a three-cup morning just to get Tommy in gear.

"Deadly weekend," Bradshaw acknowledged her with a nod, grabbing a coffee from the tray before she offered.

She stared blankly as he gulped down Tommy's three-sugared coffee without hesitating. She knew the Chief was a straight up, black, no sugar kind of guy.

"Evil doesn't take a holiday in this city." Maggie was new to the squad but not to life in the Big Apple. She was as New York as a hot pretzel with yellow mustard on a summer day at the Stadium.

Tommy grumbled as he entered the squad room. A wrinkled chambray shirt, opened at the collar, his tie all askew, made it look like he had a rough weekend. He also grabbed the wrong coffee, the one with no sugar.

"*Pffft*, what the hell is this?" Tommy gagged, spitting the taste from his lips, looking puzzled at the Dunkin' cup in his hand. "It's worse than squad coffee."

"Good morning to you too, sunshine." Maggie advised both men they'd be much better off asking the next time before grabbing anything.

The morning had barely stirred. It was quiet with just the three of them before the borough's routine street noise assaulted their environment. The century-old, beige stone and brick building, strong as a fort, stood at the corner of Simpson and East 181st Street. It was a few blocks from the El, the elevated subway line, and the tree-lined street offered little buffer to the daily din of city life for a Bronx detective.

The trio of early risers heard the gab fest between Detective Sergeant Lou Lopez and his partner Detective Hank Summers coming up the steps. Lopez bitching about why the Yanks should've gotten rid of Manager Joe Girardi two seasons ago and Summers, a Queens boy to his core, explaining how Mr. Mets, his team's bobble-headed mascot, could hit better than the Bronx Bombers.

"Good morning, fellow inmates." Summers' demeanor was cheerful as usual. "Deadly weekend in our lovely borough, eh, Chief?"

Bradshaw had failed to tell Maggie and Tommy when they arrived that their fellow officers caught a case early that morning up in Woodlawn.

"Waddya got?" Bradshaw asked, eager to get his command report and know which way the week was starting out.

Fractured

"Poor church lady," Lopez chimed in. "Looks like a push and kill.

"Strangled right inside her front door, never had a chance."

Summers explained that a priest from the nearby rectory of Saint Barnabas Church called it in after she didn't show up to make breakfast. "He'd sent an altar boy to her house after Mass. Poor kid, thirteen-years-old, still shaking when we got there. He looked in the window and saw the body."

"Something must've spooked him because the house wasn't tossed, everything as well-kept as poor old Dottie O'Neal," Lopez said, shaking his head more at the realization of how life had changed in his thirty years with the NYPD than the reality of another homicide for him to solve. The lines of decency long since erased by a generation's mores of kill or be killed, literally and figuratively.

"What makes you think the killer was a man?" Bradshaw questioned the veteran detectives.

"Poor Dottie wasn't a frail woman. She was a good, strong Irish Catholic gal standing about five-foot-nine." Summers nodded as Lopez offered his seasoned opinion. "Unlikely another woman could've overtaken her."

"That and the slight bruise marks around her windpipe look too big to have been caused by a woman's hands," Summers added for good measure. Their case rundown was soon interrupted by noise on the staircase.

"Hey, Lopez, did Daddy forget his Binky?" The guys from the Crime Scene Unit arrived back at the house making fun of the baby pacifier they had bagged and tagged at the scene.

It was enough to make Maggie's skin prickle, as if the ghost of her father had just walked through the room.

33

"What did you say?" Bradshaw turned on a dime in their direction. He remembered all too well about the killer who had terrorized women in the Big Apple fifteen years ago.

"Sorry, Chief, but there was a baby's pacifier near the body," Lopez explained.

"Not in her mouth?" Bradshaw questioned them forcefully.

"No, I mean it could've fallen out, but it was up near where her face touched the floor. Maybe it belonged to a grandkid or something."

"Get in here and close the door," Bradshaw ordered the CSU officers into the room. "That fact is not to leave this building."

"But Chief, the property clerk gets all the evidence." They were about to continue but one look at the Chief's face stopped their next syllable from fleeing their lips.

"Not one word," Bradshaw repeatedly emphatically.

Lopez, Summers and CSU zipped their lips and gestured to toss away the key not knowing how crucial it was to play this one close to the vest.

But Tommy knew…so did Maggie…and she knew what she'd have to do.

Chapter Eight

Quietly, head down, Maggie made her way to her desk in the middle of the bullpen. Eye contact would start conversation with anyone and she was all about flying solo, especially on this case. This case had been with her long before she joined the force. For years it tore her father apart and then his partner when she attended John Jay College under his instruction. This time she'd put an end to it.

"Penny for your thoughts, partner," Tommy bent over her desk, whispering in her ear. "Scratch that," he edited his train of thought. "I know what you're thinking. They caught this one, not us." He reminded her that they had enough on their plate with the dead priest in the confessional.

Tommy had become a detective just as Maggie's Dad retired and remembered how much the thought of a serial killer on the loose, on his watch, had gnawed at the old guy like a woodpecker drilling the same tree and getting nowhere.

But Tommy also knew his hot-headed partner and her burning desire not to play by the boy's rules.

"What?" Maggie looked up innocently. "I don't know what you're talking about."

"Yeah, right. Since when do you button up at the mention of an oddball killer's signature, especially that one?"

"It just hit too close to home, kinda like walking across my Dad's grave, if you know what I mean."

"I do and that's why you've gotta let it go."   Tommy reminded her how things worked around this house with each team minding their own turf.   Yet he knew she just might get burned in the process.

"This is gonna be a long, crazy summer," she recognized his warning but instinctively knew that she wouldn't heed it. "June's not here yet and it's already hotter than a branding iron on a Texas ranch."

Chapter Nine

Maggie was far from exhausted at the end of a long day, getting no further along in the clergy homicide. When your adrenalin kicks in on a major investigation, you can run for two or three days...on two or three hours' sleep a night...before crashing.

Her heart was racing faster than her old Pony car could carry her up the Saw Mill Parkway. Her head pounded with the mental gymnastics she was putting herself through, trying to merge her Dad's past with her present. The volley inside her head was exhausting as the rapid-fire energy bounced between her Dad's case and the priest's murder. To focus on only her task at hand would be expected and Maggie was anything but predictable as she pulled in front of 42 Pine Street in Yonkers.

She had called retired Detective Lieutenant Bobby Stonestreet before leaving the station and invited herself to dinner with her Godfather.

"Hold on, hold on," he yelled through the closed door as she frantically held down his buzzer, droning like the hiss of an annoying bee until you swat it. Her finger only releasing the button as he opened the door. She kissed him hello and rushed her way past him into the privacy of his river view apartment.

"Whoa, what's the rush?" He wondered. "I don't see you for a few weeks and now you're in a hurry."

"He's back, Uncle Bobby. He's back." She paced the living room in circles like a manic off her meds.

"Who's back?"

"Did you make *aglio olio with alici*?" Her nose paused to sniff her favorite dish as she sat down ready to inhale what should be savored slowly.

"Ahh, she stops to eat," he smiled, delighted in her pause to refresh. "Eat while it's hot and then we can talk."

She marveled at the way he made the pasta *al dente* and seasoned the dish to perfection with just the right amount of *pepperoncino*, just like her Dad before him.

In between bites and twirls of her fork, Maggie explained to him that the Binky Killer was back, fifteen years later.

Bobby didn't know whether to jump on the killer-hunting bandwagon or take a backseat in his retirement, enjoying the life in academia he had created for himself at the John Jay College of Criminal Justice. While he had no professional obligation to contribute to the department's investigation, this case had consumed him as much as Maggie's Dad when they were partners.

"Hey kiddo, you need to slow down and breathe." Bobby had promised her Dad he would look out for her and keep her on the straight and narrow.

"This is not your case. You need to mind the playhouse rules, especially when you're the new kid on the block."

"Uncle Bobby, you know that's not gonna happen, not with this case."

"But this case could be your last if you don't watch it," he warned her. "You've already broken the rules by even telling me what should've been kept in-house and confidential."

"But it's you. This was your case, yours and Dad's. No one knows this killer like you do."

"Well, young lady, if that was the case, we would've caught him years ago and we didn't." His reluctant admission didn't go unnoticed by Maggie.

"Not for want of trying. It consumed you both."

"And don't let it consume you too. Now, tell me about the clergy killer."

Maggie, tossing the rule book aside, revealed what little they had to go on and the frustration level that brought to bear on such a high-profile case. The case was fresh, two-day-old kind of fresh.

She washed the dishes as she talked. He sat back and sipped his merlot. He understood her need to burn off the energy while spinning the details in a round-robin game of Clue? Since she was a kid and later in college, they'd been playing a real-life version of her favorite board game with nearly every case that came before them, and now any case of hers since joining the NYPD.

"The crime scene is so contaminated with the sins of the guilty that we truly need divine intervention to discover anything substantial," she chuckled at her choice of words.

"Public places and spaces always make it hard to find valuable trace evidence. You know that," he reminded her, "which means you'll have to exercise your pretty cop brain even more." He took great pride in her accomplishments and knew her Dad was smiling down on her.

"But why do you think he's back or do you think we have a copycat?" Maggie digressed, searching for answers, wanting to solve his greatest case.

"Mags, you've gotta focus. Focus, kiddo," Stonestreet implored her. "They're watching you. Don't blow your first big case worrying about someone else's headache.

"There's no telling why his sick mind woke up again," he paused in obvious reflection, "if, in fact, it is him again."

Chapter Ten

As she climbed her front steps, she felt his presence. Was he watching her every move? Where was he hiding? What did he want from her *this* time? As many times as she tried to lock him out of her world, he always managed to creep back in, slithering like the vile asp that he was, trying to strangle her out of existence. She lived with the constant worry of psychological elimination, the reality of melting under his power, not under his control but becoming one with it. She seemed to lose her sense of self whenever he was near.

The motion sensor light lit up the front door as she slowly put her key into the lock. She always sensed him long before he intruded. It was her sixth sense. Looking over her shoulder before turning it completely, she wanted to be sure that she didn't let him in, not *this* time.

This was her time to shine.

"Cuddles, Cuddles," she called to the cat as she squeezed through the door, closing it before her furry friend could sneak out. "You'll save me, boy, won't you?" As if the cat could talk back or understand.

"You're Mommy's good boy. Yes, you are." She picked up the little fur ball and continued talking to it in a high-pitched saccharine song of infantile expressions. It was the same

41

melody which new mothers cooed at their babies. Both cats and kids looked at these ridiculous, squeaky women in wonderment of this nonsensical, ridiculous speech pattern.

Donovan watched her from the shadows and shook his head. She barely noticed him in the dark, in the recesses, in the places he didn't belong. *Stupid woman. Dumb, whiny woman,* he thought to himself. *You'd never hear a man speaking such childishness. Not a real man anyway.*

He lurked in her presence. Her focus was always on something else and not on him and that irked him. Most of the time she was oblivious to him. They reluctantly shared the same space but led different lives. Her seemingly permanent state of absentmindedness offered the perfect environment for him to move to and fro with the entry key she had given him a lifetime ago.

Donovan's madness stirred him awake with a renewed sense of purpose. Her shrill sound burned at the rear of his throat as he choked back the urge to strangle her out of existence. Hiding was getting harder. If he came out in the open...again...would she let him live? There was only one answer and he would make it right soon.

Her life since retirement had been uneventful. Other than her usual Tuesday nights at Needle Nellies, the meet-up group of lonely-hearts knitters, she didn't do much. No travel, no classes, no friends, nothing to really get her mind off him. They had been together too long and had seen too much but they couldn't dismiss each other as hard as they tried.

Having eaten dinner earlier, she refilled Cuddles' bowl with fresh water and made herself her usual nighttime elixir, Vanilla Chamomile tea. She undressed, hanging her clothes carefully on the right side of the large closet. She'd wear them again, definitely before laundering. She saved money where she could. It was essential. A woman in her position had to be ready. She couldn't rely on just a city pension and social security. There was no security in life. She learned that lesson at a young age.

She cautiously opened the drawer to her nightstand, making sure her safety net with its pearly white handle was just where she had placed it three nights earlier. Practicing on the shooting range for years made her a better shot than most cops walking a beat. Meek in demeanor. Unsuspecting in a dowdy, chunky sort of way. Not a one of them ever guessed that a killer lurked among them. Not a one of them ever cared enough to come calling now.

She turned on the TV with Cuddles in her lap as the power recliner glided her gently into relaxation. Most of the world passed her by during most of her day but she couldn't help but watch the 10 o'clock news on Fox. They always had the jump on anything exciting in the city, even though any crime story would not be a media event until eleven. That's when the cops and commissioner were always in focus at a press conference, but that was just too late for her. All hard-working people should be in bed by eleven o'clock. Nothing good happens anywhere that late at night.

"Breaking news at this hour, the holiday weekend turned even deadlier as police, this morning, discovered a church lady murdered in the Bronx."

The headline was jarring, forcing her to lift her push-button throne into its upright position. Even Cuddles jumped from her lap.

"Police say the seventy-year-old victim was discovered by an altar boy when she didn't show up to make breakfast for the priests. She had worked at the Saint Barnabas Rectory for more than twenty years." The news anchor droned on but there was no need to listen. It became the white noise of her evening. The constant hum, the buzz that made no sense to decent people.

She knew it was him. Her skin prickled at the realization that Donovan didn't like her killing Father McNamara. No, Donovan didn't like that at all. The game was on, again, but this time he wouldn't win.

Chapter Eleven

May 31st

For most people, patience was a virtue but for Maggie Flynn the virtue of knowing one's own weaknesses was her only asset at this moment. Her patience was lacking.

"This job is gonna kill you if you let it," Tommy told her to take a pause as he watched her frantic tapping of a pen on her cluttered desk, her eyes focused on the white board they hoped would lay out the killer's plan before them. "Good police work requires patience to root out the evil that knows how to burrow itself among us.

"This is different than foot patrol, kiddo," he reminded her. "It's like piecing together a jigsaw puzzle, patiently, methodically."

"Yeah, but we don't have all the pieces in front of us." She was ambitious, impetuous, anxious with the restlessness of inexperience and the idealism of youth. At thirty-years-old, Maggie didn't have the wisdom or the patience of her partner. Some things can only come with age.

"You seem overly distracted today. What's on your mind?" Tommy wondered. "You know, partners share everything."

She didn't hear him or chose to ignore him. The overhead fan teetered above her, churning the same stale air and rancid food smells which never changed at headquarters. The incessant hum of the dated fluorescent lights was the white noise which filled the space when silence was preferable, the quiet needed to think.

Maggie stared blankly at the board in front of her but her mind was surely elsewhere, like the board adjacent to theirs, the one with the church lady's homicide front and center. Maggie didn't tell him of her visit with Stonestreet but Tommy guessed her mind was on the case that gnawed at her father and was reborn with the evidence in the church lady's death.

"What wakes a sleeping killer, Tommy? What's he been doing for the past fifteen years?

"That's the real puzzle." Maggie spoke as if prioritizing the Binky case over their own homicide.

"It may be very well but it's not our puzzle to solve." Tommy frustrated that his guidance was going unheeded.

"Why this poor old lady? No family. She minded her business. Why her?"

"Maybe sheer dumb luck on the killer's part but let's get out of here." He thought taking her away from the center of the other investigation might redirect her to their task at hand, finding the clergy killer.

The front doors of the grand ninety-year-old Gothic church were still draped in the purple and black banners of mourning as was the Tolentine Rectory when they rang its doorbell. The twin spires towering over them, standing sentry, almost daring anyone to violate this space, again.

Fractured

They were invited into the front parlor where they explained to Father Flanagan why there was no usable trace evidence, making their job extremely difficult.

"In such a public place as a church, there are fingerprints on top of fingerprints," Tommy advised the sullen priest before him. His head was heavy with concern. His shoulders drooped as the banners of mourning outside.

"Hair and fibers, mixed with the street dust of hundreds of churchgoers, make the job near impossible to focus on one suspect."

"Anything you can think of, anything at all, would help us," Maggie urged the priest, still visibly shaken by his new reality. He was still trying to find forgiveness in his heart for whoever robbed him of his co-worker, his friend. Sometimes God tests you beyond your limits and this was one of those times.

"Mac, I'm sorry," he caught himself again. "I mean Father McNamara," Flanagan corrected the nickname that might have been perceived as disrespect for his colleague.

Sometimes the laity elevated clergy to such a degree that they forgot priests were people as well, with friends and family, hobbies and obligations and who enjoyed a great joke, often at their own expense.

"Father McNamara was truly looking forward to his retirement. He didn't have it in him to give any longer," Flanagan continued. "I realize that may be difficult to understand for an outsider, that a priest can't counsel any longer. But sometimes the weight of that obligation can be exhausting.

"After fifty plus years, he was ready to retire."

"Did he seem troubled by anything recently?" Tommy went through the usual litany of questions about possible enemies and events.

47

"We led a quiet life here together. We got by without sharing too much of each other's private matters.

"He always seemed like a troubled soul but that could be my projecting onto the blank, dreary canvas which I faced each morning." Flanagan now unlocking the mystery of his troubled housemate or the lonely life of one who holds the secrets of so many others, not the least of which are his own.

"It's a heavy burden to hear the daily confessions of penitents. The clergy are the delegates of Christ but who are we to confess our sins to but ourselves and God? It's not an easy load to carry." Tommy and Maggie sat silently as Flanagan relaxed into this revelation.

The detectives had both toed the line for thirteen years, from kindergarten through twelfth grade. They wore the uniform, the tartan plaid, and respected the priests and nuns who led them like lost sheep through catechism lessons. But neither of them really thought about whether priests confessed their sins to another, about whether priests had the power to face their own weaknesses in the face of another or in the face of God. Could they look another in the eye and reveal their inner demons?

"It's a struggle that Saint Nicholas Tolentino postulated more than seven-hundred-fifty years ago and one that plagues many priests to this day." Flanagan went on to quote the church's namesake: *The heavens are not pure in the sight of Him whom I serve; how then shall I, a sinful man, stand before Him?*

Such grand questions on life and inner strife had never faced the three of them as profoundly as they had today.

"I guess the darkest secrets are hidden in the most unlikely places," Maggie conceded as they thanked Father Flanagan for his candor and assistance and realized that evil

Fractured

confessed may be evil unchecked if never to be discovered in the light of day outside the confessional.

Chapter Twelve

June 5th

A cool breeze ruffled her billowy skirt as she stood on the corner of Martha Avenue and East 241st Street looking up at the stone steps of the old home. Goodness lived there or at least that's what everyone thought on this residential street where the only things older than the church were the mighty oak trees. The well-established Saint Barnabas Church offered the blessed goodness sought by those suffering the routine evils of life. That was her old reality but no longer. She grabbed the reins of this new life with her first kill and wouldn't stop until the sinful misery was back in its box.

She steadied herself for the task ahead of her this morning. She had seen the job posting online this morning...along with Dottie O'Neal's obituary, poor soul. She'd put it right...soon!

"Good morning," she greeted the priest humbly as he opened the door to his angel of death. Her tidy dated appearance belied her true intentions. She was as plain as shredded wheat in an empty bowl and her curly bob made her salt and pepper hair look exactly like a frayed Brillo pad. He

Fractured

was as unsuspecting as a child in his mother's arms, unthreatened by the evil hidden before him disguised in a tightly buttoned blouse and worn floral skirt at least twenty-five years out of fashion.

She knew the rectory at Saint Barnabas needed to replace its dead housekeeper and she wanted to be the first in line for the job. First in line for the interview. First in line to secure her place. First in line to correct the never-ending litany of mistakes. Woe to anyone who tried to eradicate the scourge she was compelled to rain down to wash away years of hurt.

"Good morning," he acknowledged her with a smile, inviting her into the seemingly safe haven. "You're an early bird," Father Wojcick acknowledged that they had only placed an ad in the Sunday church bulletin and the local newspaper the day before. He assumed he'd have a bunch of emailed applications to review this morning, never expecting anyone to just ring the doorbell.

He invited her into the church office. The gloominess of the room's dark olive and brown décor, unchanged in at least thirty years, was made more somber by window shades that were never lifted. Was it to keep the outside from looking in or the inside from escaping?

"I only just finished the seven o'clock Mass in the downstairs chapel," he explained that he needed to clean it up a bit. "The altar boys had to run back to class and we're short-staffed here at the rectory. So, I'm managing everything."

"It was a tragedy what happened to your housekeeper, killed like that in her own home." She offered sincere sympathy for the fate that had claimed an unsuspecting life, unguarded in her own sanctuary. She could empathize with a woman left unprotected, innocent and alone.

51

Father Wojcick acknowledged the world had become a dark place, as he suggested that someone should've escorted Dottie O'Neal home that fateful night.

"We ran that program jointly with the Presbyterian Church. Dottie had volunteered for years.

"This used to be a safe neighborhood," he continued but she disregarded his feeble attempt to shirk the duty he owed to her, the duty he owed to Dottie.

"Do you live nearby?" He wondered.

"Close enough," she stated without revealing too much.

The interview was routine, smoothly moving from job responsibilities to background history. She'd be expected to prepare morning and midday meals, clean both the rectory and the chapel downstairs and generally tidy up after Wojcick and the other priest who resided there over the weekends.

She listened and responded patiently to his questions. She was in no hurry. He'd be going nowhere soon, very, very soon.

"Can you show me around?" She asked, explaining that she'd want to understand the full scope of expectations. She really wanted him to lead the way, to steer her through any church security systems and map her escape route.

"We're very basic here." Wojcick showed her the only iPad which ran an app for the front entry's video doorbell. "The doorbell chimes throughout the rectory and in the sacristy behind the chapel downstairs, but we need to be here in the office to actually see who's at the door and then decide whether to buzz them in. It's the world we live in now. It's how I first saw you this morning."

Kaching! She could easily delete the video files on her way out.

"Mrs. Delaney, the church secretary, works from ten to two on Tuesdays, Thursdays and Fridays. But that schedule

52

seems to change as Mrs. Delaney seems to change," he smiled, revealing that Mrs. Delaney liked to grab a trip on the casino bus at least twice a month.

She smiled back knowing that no one was showing up this Monday to save him from damnation.

"Most weekdays the altar boys clean up the lower chapel before heading back to class. So, you'd basically just need to tidy up the rooms down here, the office, the kitchen and the front parlor where I meet with parishioners.

"I manage to take care of myself in the residence upstairs."

But you couldn't take care of Dottie O'Neal, could you? She thought to herself.

"Let me show you downstairs," he said before leading her through the kitchen, past the laundry-room and down the rickety wooden back stairs.

As they made their way into the basement, she saw the entrance to the chapel on the left and wondered about the door just to the right of the small sacristy.

"Ahh, that's the secret of every altar boy for the past hundred years," he said as he opened the portal to the mysterious chasmal space ahead. He told her that when the Italianate church and the adjacent elementary school were built, they connected the church and rectory to the school. "It's quite convenient when it's snowing outside," he smiled.

Well, she'd wiped that smile right off his face with a quick shot to the heart from the rear.

He died thinking she wanted a job when what she really sought was a lifetime's retribution. Since he had mentioned everyone's schedule, she knew he'd just lay in a pool of his own ooze until at least tomorrow. Pearl's silencer kept this secret tunnel from echoing the sound of death and she was gone as quickly as she had entered his life.

Chapter Thirteen

June 6th

"I haven't been in church as much in the past fifteen years as I've been in the past three weeks," Martin greeted an officer on the scene with a lift of his coffee cup. Maggie pulling up in her silver blue beauty raised a few eyebrows. The patrolmen on scene wondered how a new, young detective got to drive a classic Mustang while they could barely afford to send their kids to Catholic school.

"Let me guess, inside the tunnel?" She asked, suspecting the inevitable.

"Yeah, how did you know?" Tommy was amazed at her early morning insight.

"We used to live in Woodlawn," she told him. "Every kid around knew about the legendary tunnel."

They climbed the front stairs two at a time, crisscrossing their way between the crowd of officers, forensic and medical examiner personnel, even school administrators. They all crowded the small cascade of steps leading to the rectory's front door in shock and awe. Who would, who could kill a priest? Inside a rectory? So close to God? So many people, so few answers.

Fractured

They made their way into the secret tomb of Father Wojcick careful to ease their way among the so-called officials crowded inside. Everyone seems to want a piece of the deadly pie when murder happens. Why is that? Investigators should make it a priority to clear the scene of riff-raff and contamination instead of giving in to everyone who thinks it's their case.

Tommy, especially, knew the harm which could result from the power struggle over a case. After twenty-five years on the job, he'd seen too many investigations go up in flames because of detectives fighting to get another win on their belt or officers sullying the crime scene while evidence goes missing.

He wondered if the brass would yield authority over the case and call in the FBI. Any small town would need to call in the feds but this was New York City. They could handle anything.

Surely, all bets would be off if the city did call in the FBI to investigate the priest killings. There's that unwritten rule of three. One more and they'd have a serial killer on their hands.

Maggie stopped just outside the threshold to the tunnel as if entering the devil's lair. She inhaled deeply. Since her school days she had wondered about the myths and legendary tales about this subterranean tunnel, the escape route for kids to cut class or better yet the secret passage for romantic trysts...between the priests and nuns in the convent. Little minds create big legends. Her mind now focused on the new narrative unfolding before them, who's killing priests in the Bronx and why?

"Two priests in two weeks in the same precinct is not a coincidence," Tommy stating the obvious. Maggie had become more than his sounding board since starting the job. She was a real contributing partner and he hoped the vocal volley would spur them in a new direction toward the killer

"No, it's not and it just happens to be four blocks from where the church lady was killed," Maggie giving herself reason to explore the connection against all departmental inclinations.

This scene was cleaner than the first, Maggie and Tommy both realized as they crouched near the lifeless body. No brain matter desecrated the walls as in the hallowed space of the confessional. Poor Father Wojcick dropped where he was shot and a small pool of blood gathered under his chest.

This time the fatal shot was a through and through wound close to the heart. So, since the bullet wasn't lodged inside the body, then it should be in the walls, the furniture, some friggin' thing inside the tunnel with maybe a fragment left inside the victim's chest.

Tommy walked behind the priest's body and stood where his feet were pointed downward, as if he fell face first after being shot. The priest's body had already been rolled onto his back, probably by some over-zealous probie officer. The newbies seemed to be repelled or baffled by dead bodies, wanting to make sure the guy's really dead despite the massive pool of blood under the body.

"The killer came up behind him," Maggie now stating the obvious. After all, if Wojcick had looked his killer in the eye, he would've likely hunched over, probably falling to his side. His knees would have buckled under him, taking his last breath before collapsing onto the cold, lifeless surface. Instead, he took one in the back and dropped to his death face down.

"You'd never find this tunnel unless you knew about it or unless the good padre invited you in," said Tommy.

Fractured

"So, it's either someone from the parish, someone he knew or both." Maggie continued explaining that even while many parishioners suspected there was a tunnel, very few believed it and even fewer had ever walked its path.

Wojcick was about five-foot-eleven, not a short man, and took a bullet just below his left scapula and almost spot on the heart. A clean shot from close range and probably someone close to his height. Had the killer been much shorter than Wojcick, the gun would've been shot upwards, meaning the bullet could've ricocheted anywhere, even inside the body, through the lungs, tearing through the heart, maybe even shredding the brain before making its way out...if it made its way out.

Tommy was about the same height as Wojcick and stood as a test for them to divide the room into searchable quadrants. Maggie and Tommy narrowed the space, hoping to find the deadly bullet, hoping to link it back to McNamara's killer. Yet, when they traced the bullet's trajectory from Tommy's chest level to the wall in front of him, all they found was a scar on the wall dead ahead.

"Look at this," Maggie calling him over. "Damn stone wall is barely nicked." The hundred-year-old tunnel absorbed the impact of the bullet which bounced off the wall leaving a white scratch on the mottled grey slab.

Tommy looked at his feet, as if expecting to find the bullet waiting for him, saying, *"Here I am, come and get me."*

What they did find was a smudge in the dust layered on the rarely used corner of the floor.

"This killer is smart. No bullet, no prints, nothing to trace except a scar on the wall and a streak on a dirty floor." Maggie frustrated that this trail was cool before it even started.

"I'll call the CSU guys over here," Tommy said. "Maybe they can tell us from a print of the wall mark what caliber could make that particular striation." It was a stretch and he knew it.

But they did have McNamara's bullet and if the caliber of this one matched that, then they could at least link the two in some small aspect, other than the fact that they were both priests in the Bronx.

Father Jan Wojcick was the antithesis of Father McNamara. Where McNamara was discontent, a real curmudgeon nearing retirement, Wojcick was a lively presence in the parish. He was often found shooting hoops with the kids on the playground after school. He brought back guitars to Mass and modernized what had become a stodgy, but large, active Irish-Catholic parish in the Archdiocese. The principal was devastated. And Mass, much to the chagrin of Cardinal Donohue downtown, was canceled for the next three days, at least until Wojcick's funeral.

Maggie and Tommy made their way back above ground into Father Wojcick's private office. They searched his desk, scoping out any connections, emails, phone messages, anything to reveal why he opened the door to his angel of death this morning. The search for a new rectory housekeeper was obvious after Dottie O'Neal's death with ads running in the church bulletin and neighborhood newspapers but no one knew if he had started canvassing candidates so early in the day.

"Check this out," Maggie called Tommy over as she had been reading the priest's emails on the iPad left powered on atop his desk. "There's an app on here for the video doorbell out front. Maybe we have a clear shot at a suspect."

Tommy took it upon himself to call the doorbell company only to discover that the app itself only streams live video. Storing video files from the device is a premium feature and the church didn't subscribe to anything premium. Any hope of a stored mugshot of the clergy killer would be a virtual miracle.

They asked the officer outside to ring the doorbell. As he obliged, his face popped up on Wojcick's iPad but was gone in sixty seconds. Clearly, without any signs of a break-in, Wojcick didn't feel threatened by the image on his screen just moments before his death. He said hello to his final goodbye.

Chapter Fourteen

The bright sun was high in the sky this late spring day. Yet a cool breeze still caused Maggie to shiver as she stepped into the warmth. Tommy too. He tried to shake off the scene inside. Murder was a brutal business and cops had to be detached to do their job effectively but some kills, some murders, unnerved even the most seasoned detective.

A crowd had formed on the sidewalk outside the rectory, on the small corner of Martha Avenue across the street. Maggie and Tommy eyed the faces in the crowd, from side to side, as if a killer lurked among them. Tall, short, man, woman, kids, nuns. How do you know? Does a killer wear his sin on his sleeve like a merit badge?

They walked under the yellow crime scene tape which now blocked passage directly across East 241st Street, just beyond the school yard where two officers had been posted. The kids would spend recess inside today. Sadly, this was one school year they'd always remember for all the wrong reasons.

She never forgot a face. She watched them walk toward their cars. She took shelter among the minions. This was in her own backyard, so she had to be careful, very careful, especially knowing the cops on the scene would be searching the crowd for suspects so close to the time of death.

She saw them, both of them, as soon as the door to the rectory opened. Oh yes, she'd have to be very careful now.

Chapter Fifteen

*N*ice going, idiot, Donovan whispered to himself as he followed her home. *People you know showing up at the crime scene. Great way to get us caught.*

She sensed his presence as he stepped at her heels, crowding her thoughts, jamming her life in too many ways. She needed an escape, from him and from too many curious onlookers causing a bottleneck on this busy little corner of the Bronx.

Too much noise in the ethers for her. She wasn't used to it in her lonely little world of knitting and needlework, cats and doilies. Yet, now that she had a taste of the attention, she liked it. She had a little pep in her step as she walked up bustling McLean Avenue toward her apartment on Sterling Hill. Life in the spotlight gave her a reason to get out of bed in the morning. It gave her a reason to kill...again.

Donovan was enjoying his ability to move in and out of her life incognito. She would see him, feel him, only when he chose. At least, that's what he thought. He wondered, as he walked, what went on in that pea-sized brain of hers. What made her think she could compete with his success? Did she really think she could beat him at his own game?

She imagined she was keeping him at bay just long enough to get her skills perfected for her greatest kill and final release. She didn't feed his frenzy and the deep need he had to be heard. His gruff voice was like a butcher's knife cutting through her life in ways she never dreamed. She thought it better to remain quiet. Don't chat him up. Don't acknowledge his presence. He's a fool...she was sure...to think there was weakness in her silence. His biggest mistake would be to underestimate her.

Donovan picked up a newspaper on the way home and laughed at the front page.

"*The Unforgiveable Sin*" heralded Dottie O'Neal's death across the Daily News' cover.

Another fake news headline when the real story was just blocks away. *How do newspapers keep up with Twitter these days?* He laughed to himself as getting into the rhythm of a 21st Century news cycle took some adjusting for him. Fifteen years ago, the lead that bleeds usually came in the morning paper, echoed by morning TV. Now, everything was online and instantaneous...and anonymous. Hunting lonely-hearts had never been so easy.

He sipped his coffee dark and straight. No almond or skim milk, no sugar, no fancy latte for him. He considered himself a straight shooter in a mixed-up world of people suffering identity crises en masse. The world got so fucked up so fast. If he could help purge society of some of these screwballs, he'd be doing everyone a favor, everyone except her.

She was his primary target now, but he'd need a little practice and a whole lot of patience first. Even he knew he was a bit rusty. The Dottie O'Neal kill was too spontaneous for him.

If Donovan was anything, he was methodical, not impulsive. He wasn't rash despite how others characterized him all those years ago. Like a big game hunter, he stalked his prey carefully, knowing that one false move, one slip into the light, one surveillance camera unseen could be the end of his sport.

He powered on his MacBook on the kitchen table, choosing to ignore her. Her lips moved in his direction but she said nothing he wanted to hear. They stayed clear of each other in a reluctant détente, fuming with an inner turmoil, gathering steam until the next eruption.

He purchased his new computer as soon as the sales geek in Best Buy told him Mac is dope! Only the best for Donovan. Anything to make his job easier, no matter the cost.

He truly had done his homework since Father McNamara was gunned down. He needed to quickly learn a new way to hide his steps, make himself untraceable to compete with her. Maybe he taught her how to kill and whet her appetite for the spotlight but he was the master. Remaining anonymous had been the key to his success all these years.

Donovan had registered at no less than three anonymizer websites. They allowed him to log in online from New York and appear to be in Germany, Turkey, Greece, even the Middle East for fuck's sake. No traceable footprint when his new identity as Sam Smith chatted up his next victim in any one of the many lonely-hearts stitch and bitch groups online. Sam could be a man or a woman and his unknowing targets didn't need to be certain until their face-to-face encounter.

Fractured

Sam was just as disconnected as the rest of the knitters on the Net, looking for friendship in a webbed world of knitting. *Let's meet for coffee, dear,* he laughed to himself at how gullible most of this pool of pansies were despite all the warnings blathered by every feature and crime reporter on a slow news day. Too naïve to understand the dangers of life in the cyber age and gullible enough to be his prime targets.

He realized that all this surfing was more time-consuming, at first, but it made the task of zeroing in so much smoother. Not only could he develop a friendly rapport with these women, but he could find out where they lived, and the nearest security cameras positioned around their neighborhoods all from the comfort of home.

While he locked on a target, she was just getting started.

Chapter Sixteen

June 7th

"Who knew *we'd* be sharing morning coffee with Cardinal Richard Donohue, two of the city's outstanding lapsed Catholics," Tommy said, his voice dripping with sarcasm as they headed down the Deegan Expressway toward midtown Manhattan. Donohue had only been in residence about a year as New York's top Catholic cleric and had a few scandals and economic woes already piling up before priests started dropping like flies.

The massive church complex for Saint Patrick's Cathedral stretched from Madison to Fifth Avenues, from 50th to 51st Streets, flanked by the Saks Fifth Avenue Department Store and the Armani Exchange boutique. This was certainly midtown's high rent district.

Tommy pulled into a No Parking Zone heading west on 51st Street, just one of the perks of being a detective on assignment in the big city. Ignore the red and white warning signs and park wherever crime struck! Maybe that's why the city's crimefighters drove cars that looked like they'd been run over by a Zamboni during half-time at Madison Square Garden.

They cautiously rang the doorbell at 460 Madison Avenue, the Archdiocese's official address, granting entry to the majestic home of Cardinal Donohue. New York's legendary police department and the city's Catholic Church had a long history together, dating back to its Irish roots in the late 19th Century. After all, its first bishop, Richard Luke Concanen, was Irish-born. But the luck of the Irish was clearly in short supply right now.

A young woman answered the door. She was demure but polished and professional. She wore a well-tailored navy skirt suit with a peplum jacket, stylish but all business. Maggie eyed the comfortable rubber-soled shoes which contradicted the put-together outfit, probably from Saks on the corner. She pictured the quiet secretary in this place of religious pomp and circumstance. Or was she an executive assistant now in the 21st Century? Anyway, she imagined the shoes were to maintain the quiet dignity of the church headquarters in New York or to preserve its historic wood floors, maybe both.

The young assistant invited the detectives into a cozy sitting room inside the rectory. Large neo-Gothic windows lit the wood-paneled library with bright light. The thick glass panes dimmed the noise from busy Madison Avenue. An intricately woven Persian-style area rug stretched into nearly every nook and cranny while salmon colored, velvet-cushioned mahogany side-chairs tempted guests to sit before their audience with the Cardinal.

"Detectives Flynn and Martin, good to see you again," said Ray Peretti, extending his hand in a cordial greeting as he entered the room. "The Cardinal's quite anxious to understand what's happening to our priests."

As they rose to greet Peretti, Cardinal Donohue came rushing in like a tenured professor late to his own lecture. Imposing at six-foot-three-inches tall, robust and full of energy. He certainly wasn't a meek disciple who needed a pulpit to have his voice heard over a crowd. He was a busy, powerful man in New York and this inconvenience was keeping him from managing the church's two-hundred-fifty-million dollars' worth of assets and serving the city's three-million parishioners.

"Detectives, good day," he too offered Maggie and Tommy the obligatory welcome. But they knew better. For them this was just like being summoned to the principal's office. They feared the Cardinal almost as much as being called down to One Police Plaza to face a possible rip, looking at a month-long "reduction in pay" for insubordination.

"What are you doing to catch this guy who's killing our priests? They're terrified up in the Bronx." The Cardinal got right down to business. He had no time to waste because hours clicked away toward another murder.

"Your Eminence, we want to find this killer as much as you do," Tommy, being the senior detective on the case, tried to assuage the prelate's concerns.

"Right now, there's not a lot to go on. No trace evidence, no weapon and no apparent motive."

"But my priests are dropping like flies. No one wants to say Mass at Tolentine and Barnabas. That's a big problem for us," Cardinal Donohue vented the issues from his managerial perch.

"Everyone is fearful, from priests to sisters to parishioners and school kids," he continued, shaking his head. His little red skull cap unflappable but weary with the weight of scandal.

"And we have good men facing death for no apparent reason," Peretti chimed in as if to make the church's concern focus more on the victims rather than the business at hand.

"Mr. Peretti, believe me when I tell you that we've been working non-stop since Memorial Day and we won't stop until we arrest someone," Maggie tried to add a softer touch to the tension in the room. "We can only do our best with what little we have."

"This brings all the wrong kind of attention right to our doorstep and the Vatican is not too happy." Cardinal Donohue shared his frustration at not being able to protect his flock. "Everyone in a collar is considered a suspect for the terrible deeds of a sanctioned few," he referenced the church's troubled past. "This time, priests are the victims and we don't know why."

"Maybe you can have the priests in the Bronx ask parishioners to come forward with even the slightest bit of information," Tommy suggested, clearly wanting to steer the discussion away from the past sex abuse scandal that rocked the church to its core. He knew there was no link to it right now, until they had more. Yet Tommy also knew in his gut that the media and the city's Catholics would always be wondering. "Maybe place the request in the church bulletin, give them our anonymous tip line to call with information.

"We're grabbing at straws here and the only thing that links them is they were both Catholic priests in the Bronx," Tommy said. The detectives could not let themselves be sidetracked to revisit past scandals and crimes when a killer was already scoping out his next victim for a nefarious reason that only he knew.

"Ray, that's a good idea about spreading the word with the tip line," Cardinal Donohue agreed, his position less abrasive than ten minutes earlier. "It's only Wednesday. We can get a special rush printing for Tolentine and Barnabas this Sunday and have the other Bronx parishes alert the congregants.

"Detectives, thank you for coming down here. I know it takes you away from the search at hand and we do appreciate it.

69

I do appreciate it," he emphasized. The Cardinal left the room as quickly as he entered on to solve the next crisis in his day.

Fractured

Chapter Seventeen

June 9th

"You think this has anything to do with the never-ending sex abuse complaints that seem to face the church?" Maggie didn't think so but felt compelled to raise the specter of scandal.

"Nah, this is very personal," Tommy certain in his beliefs as they descended the steps of Mt. Olympus back into the fracas of midtown. "If this was a political statement, the killer would make it very public. On the other hand, if he was a victim of abuse, he'd go after just his attacker and most likely stop."

"So, we've got a guy hunting down priests and we don't know why. There's only one way to play this," Maggie paused and looked at her partner. "Dinner and a game of Clue."

"What the fuh…"

She cut Tommy short. "You greet a Cardinal with that mouth?" She teased him, stopping him before he uttered the most banal of all modern curse words.

She explained that Clue was her favorite game when she was a kid and because her Dad was a detective, they got into a routine of playing a real-life game with every case he brought home. Of course, the gruesome details were watered down for her young ears but she relished helping her Dad discover whether Miss Peacock really did it in the library with a pipe.

"My Godfather has taken over the role of protagonist, so I bounce everything off him and we play while we eat," she explained that's where Italians do their best thinking...and debating...across the dinner table. She called her Uncle Bobby and told him to expect two.

"I had no idea that your Godfather was Bobby Stonestreet," Tommy said as they pulled into a spot in front of his building, "...or that he lived in the Son of Sam building." They both laughed.

"Talk about having a serial killer under your roof." Tommy's sarcastic humor was not lost on Maggie. Most men found her intelligence and wit attractive because she could follow their often-cryptic clues to rationalize almost anything.

"Well, hello, come on in," Bobby was waiting for them and knew in advance what to expect...a night full of clues to hunt down a monster.

"I hope you like clams oreganato and linguini with calamari." Bobby's query was directed at Tommy because he knew Maggie's appetite would gobble almost anything he made.

"Are you sure this is Yonkers and not Little Italy?" Tommy asked with a smile wider than a cannoli.

They didn't realize how ravenous they were until they sat down.

The dining room had a sweeping view of the Hudson River through its sliding doors to the terrace. It was cozy and intimate, not well-appointed but typical for a retired bachelor. Perfectly proportioned for the lively discussion and game ahead.

Fractured

"We had an interesting afternoon with the Cardinal." Maggie explained that she felt reprimanded by him for not doing a good job but pushed on to do better.

"They teach them that in the seminary," Tommy suggested. "Teach your children well and then tell them to do better."

Bobby understood the Cardinal's extreme concern and Maggie's insecurities on such a high-profile case. He also knew Tommy had been around the block once or twice and hoped he would guide his beloved goddaughter while teaching her the rules of the playground. He was very happy to realize that the Binky Killer wasn't up for discussion tonight.

Maggie explained the rules of their real-life, verbal game to Tommy and offered to go first.

"I think our suspect did it in the confessional with a nine-millimeter gun."

"I think our suspect is a man," Bobby suggested as Tommy caught the rhythm of these mental gymnastics.

"Prove it," Maggie said, knowing full well that's all that really mattered when trying to catch a killer.

Bobby explained to both of them that shooting isn't typical for female serial killers who prefer poison, but he was bothered by the use of a nine-millimeter gun which is relatively small for a man's hand.

"But it's affordable, maybe our guy is cheap." Tommy was truly enjoying himself here more than the usual circle-jerking that went on in the squad room.

"I think our guy has some military or police training," Maggie continued the round-robin of clues. "He's clean, more than tidy, and his kills are always direct hits."

"You're hunting and he knows how to hide his tracks well, so you may be right." Bobby knew after forty years on the job, the last twenty-five as a detective, killers always have a pattern."

"The kills are purposeful, almost vengeful, which makes each of them very personal," Tommy explaining that the military precision of each shot meant the priests had a target on their back.

"The only link is that our vics were both priests in the Bronx, so we're grasping at straws here," Maggie frustrated that this true crime was much harder to figure out than any childhood game.

Their minds were working the same case from different directions. Maggie and Tommy, they were a study in contrasts. She was new and eager. He was older and jaded. She was stylish, even on the job. He was rumpled and always looked like the iron broke after the dog dragged his clothes across the floor. Maggie was impetuous and flew by the seat of her pants. Tommy was more laid back, displaying the patience and wisdom of an earned intuition, like the sage now before them.

"Then the link is between your killer and each victim whom he chooses for his own reason," Bobby stating the obvious but sometimes that's the only path to certainty. "If it's not abuse, then figure out the motive and you'll find your killer."

Maggie needed to refuel with another shot of espresso as they continued this mental exercise.

"She can be hotheaded at times and she gets easily frustrated, so you've gotta keep an eye on her," Stonestreet urged Tommy to look out for Maggie because he knew all too well how she could go off the rails. "Her ambition sometimes forces her ahead of the pack. She's smart, very smart, but modesty comes hard."

Fractured

"What are you two smirking at?" She wondered as she returned from the kitchen to refill their wine glasses, her mug-sized espresso cup in hand.

"Good God, why don't you have A/C in this place?" She barked while wafting her collar away from her neck. The evening did nothing to cool the early climate change of the springtime heatwave.

"Maybe you're going through the changes," Tommy joked and she snapped her head in a 180-degree turn from her outdoor perch now on the patio. "Welcome to the heat of Major Cases."

"Only a month together?" Stonestreet laughed. "Yes, you're going to make a fine pair." He was certain that she was in good hands.

Chapter Eighteen

June 10th

Donovan climbed the steps to Our Lady of Mount Carmel Church. He took them easily two at a time, looking for the Saturday night meeting of lonely-hearts in this Belmont neighborhood. How it had changed in the fifty or so years since Dion and the Belmonts sang on its street corners. Now, the once Italian neighborhood was truly ethnically diverse except for the market where Italian-Americans converged at the holidays for baccalà and homemade lasagna.

He couldn't do much to hide his appearance since the heatwave continued. To wear a hooded anything or an androgynous puffer coat would really attract more attention than he wanted. Signs pointed to the meeting room around the corner from the main church so he descended the steps and slunk into a back seat in the gathering place.

Donovan was anything but shy but it was a role he fell into easily to lure his prey. After years of hunting these desperate victims, he knew they thrived on taking care of the bashful, withdrawn newcomers, bringing them into the fold and he obliged.

Tonight, it really was a social gathering more than a stitchery group or a bingo game. These ladies gathered for a

Fractured

weekly gab fest. Some knitted while others played cards and they all seemed to enjoy the buffet of homemade baked goods. Donovan, on the other hand, turned his nose at anything made in someone else's kitchen. After all, how do you know if they licked the spoon before stirring or whether their damn cat walked across the counter as they baked. *Hair in the mix. Disgusting!*

It didn't take long for Maureen Lasher to approach him and give him a warm introduction. Donovan introduced himself as Sam and explained that he felt out of place but she dismissed his feigned insecurity and said she expected some husbands to show up, eventually, because they all wanted to nibble at the buffet. *Don't we all,* he thought to himself.

"Are you new to Belmont? I've never seen you on the Avenue."

Donovan kept his answers short. *Yes, no, not really.*

"I come here just to get out of the house. It gets lonely when you live alone."

So easy to talk to, so free to share information. *Stupid woman.*

"Same for me." He knew common ground always drew women together in a weird camaraderie, establishing a foundation of trust with perfect strangers.

"Maybe we can grab a bite after the meeting," Maureen suggested. "Heck, I live so close, we should just go to my place and I'll whip up something."

That's right, dear one. Invite a strange man home, someone you've just met, brilliant idea. He loved it. Sam was a welcome visitor.

Maureen felt so naughty sneaking out of their little meeting early, yet barely anyone looked up from their isolated preoccupation.

The early evening humidity finally cracked under pressure and they exited into a much-needed downpour. Of course, Maureen had an umbrella with her. She was always ready for whatever came her way.

Even death? He wondered.

"Oh, we can both fit under here," she politely offered cover to her new friend.

Yeah, sure we can, as the metal spokes, acting like gargoyles, directed a steady trickle of water dripping down his shirt as they walked up East 187th Street toward Maureen's apartment.

What am I doing? He thought to himself. *You should know better.*

"You know, Maureen, I think I'll just head home. It's not a night to be out without an umbrella." He coughed for added effect, giving his rough voice a new sickly edge.

"Oh, dear, maybe another time," she suggested, offering him her umbrella to take with him as they neared her front stoop. He declined the wet, sloppy mess.

"I'm here every Saturday."

Yeah, right, like I'd be dumb enough to come back. He enjoyed his silent conversations with himself. They always made perfect sense.

He was losing patience, especially now, especially with himself. The rain pounded his raw edges but instead of beating him down, it energized him like a Vichy shower. He was eager to kill but this seemed sloppy, even for him. Too many witnesses, too much chatting, too much unrehearsed could get him too dead instead.

78

Chapter Nineteen

June 11th

Sunday mornings had suddenly become more tense since she decided to play his game.

She kills a few priests and thinks what she's done! He thought to himself.

His leisure time was violated by his whiny shadow. She was nowhere and everywhere. Photos of Mom and her crowded every flat surface as dust and cat hair piled up around them. Move one framed photo just an inch and see the outline, just like the chalk around a body at a crime scene. The outline of a life snuffed out.

As many times as she dusted, he coughed up a nagging hairball of disgust. His entire life was spent living in her shadow. It was time for him to cut the cord. Time for him to break free. No more sneaking around. He needed to man up, take charge, live his life, not hers.

He turned the pages of the New York Times but could barely focus on reading. So vast was the paper's contents, yet devoid of anything to hold his interest. He sat with his breakfast of deli coffee, black, straight up and stale cigarettes. The puke green Formica table stained and burned by the retinue of men before him. She held onto it as a link to Mom. The dank, putrid air smelled like a drunk in a dark alley perfumed by cheap tobacco and urine. He was immune. His lifeless soul held no windows to the outside…or to the past.

Donovan was preoccupied this morning. The foreign sensation violated his usual sense of order, his laser-driven purpose, to get the attention he craved and so deserved. His desire, which she had forced into submission several years ago, was now free to end this tug-o-war between them. He was the dominant and would force her into total submission…if not complete annihilation.

Last night could have been a disaster. He needed to forget Maureen Lasher and move on to a new hunting ground. He should have known better than to be so sloppy near Arthur Avenue. Killing old church ladies there gets noticed and that can get you caught. There's street justice in that neighborhood where everyone has known everyone else's business for decades.

Yet the urge to feed his deadly hunger was growing at a speed and in a way that was new to him. This time she was pushing him, driving him, forcing his hand into sloppiness. Maybe she wants him to get caught.

She wants to get rid of me. She thinks if I'm out of the way, then she can go back to living her quiet, pathetic existence.

It's the dawn of a new week, baby, think again.

He spent the rest of his day hunting online. Cyber Sistas, Stitch & Bitch, Needle Nellies, Draw & Pour.

Good Lord, why do these imbeciles think up these names? Why do so many women think they need some cutesy little name to get together?

All men need is a TV and a six pack to hang out. He laughed to himself, realizing that he never had a band of brothers or close friends. His voice, his screams, often echoed in a chamber of isolation.

They shared the same space but lived in different worlds. His loneliness anchored her in a grey morass, growing worse. His headaches. Her frustration. Her voice was his echo. He couldn't breathe. He shook it off and got on with things. He'd done it before. She clung to the past and stewed in her restlessness. He focused on today and plotted his next move.

Tension filled their space, hung in the air, pulled at the energy in opposite directions to the point of shredding it to pieces. This was no way for them to live but it was the only reality they knew. The only reality they had ever known. A shared path to oblivion.

She disappeared into the heat and Donovan could breathe easier alone at home. He enjoyed his cyber hunting ground among the faithful without her looking over his shoulder. He generally found an open door to friendship among church congregants. For whatever their reasons, people who went to church routinely seemed more amenable to welcoming new folks into their midst.

Donovan focused on the area around the Immaculate Conception Church on Gun Hill Road. He was doing his homework this time. He loved the Internet, allowing him to map his kill zone from the safety of his own home, in the living room they shared...when she wasn't around. The Net offered street view maps, displaying the alleys and corners near the church, while the city's transportation department listed the exact location of traffic cameras.

Cars and criminals, even the elevated subway line, now had a stranglehold on this corner of Williamsbridge. A hundred years ago when Immaculate Conception was built, its yellow brick majesty towered over a working-class neighborhood surrounded by vacant farm land. Now, urban sprawl squeezed out any sense of a genteel existence. The church now slumps just blocks away from a high school where metal detectors greet students at the door. Immaculate Conception had certainly weathered a cyclone of changes in its time on Earth, almost as much as Donovan.

He zoomed in for a closer look but it was hard to tell from the Internet's street view maps whether it was floodlights or cameras that were mounted just above the church's red side-door. The back of the church faced the front of the rectory in the rear of the parking lot. Secure cover seemed possible on the steps leading to the church's lower level. The apartment buildings on the adjacent corner and across the street were also likely to have security cameras. Donovan would canvas the area by daylight tomorrow. He was on top of his game but you could never be too careful when playing to kill.

In searching online meetup groups he discovered that the parish elementary school hosted networking events for foodies, single parents, Salsa Saturdays, and yes, Needle Nellies. He joined one meetup, through his usual anonymizer sites, allowing him to create his online profile virtually untraceable. Better to leave no breadcrumbs when traveling the path to hell.

Donovan didn't want to befriend someone too chatty in the group because their social tentacles had a broad reach. He'd rather have someone who posted occasionally but with few friends in their circle. At least they'd be likely to befriend a new member without bragging to everyone. Besides, he'd make sure they'd stay quiet as they took their last breath.

"Hi Serena, I'm new and thought I'd come to Friday night's meetup. Can you tell me more about the group?" He sent her a private chat message and waited like a patient panther, ready to pounce once the stage was set and secure.

Fractured

It didn't take Serena Gomez long to reply. She was eager to share the meetup's information with this stranger named Sam. She told him that the group was mainly Spanish-speaking women, with one or two older men, who enjoyed getting together mostly to chat in a safe place but also to embroider and knit. Serena said he would be most welcome this weekend and she looked forward to meeting him.

That would give Donovan a week to cultivate Sam's rapport with Serena. The buildup was foreplay to the big reveal Friday night. He'd even bone up on his Spanglish to make her feel more at ease. Her naiveté made her more vulnerable to monsters like him.

When you're alone and trolling the Internet, it becomes your main link to social interaction. There's a burning impulse to check it constantly. We all want someone to know that we exist, that we're alive...at least for now.

Chapter Twenty

June 16th

"Serena, dear, I'm babysitting for a neighbor on Friday," he offered up a benign lie, something she'd buy, something she'd easily understand for his excuse not to show his face in the group. "Can we get together after your meetup? I'll be done by nine."

She agreed to meet him at the coffee shop on the tiny peninsula across from the church. Donovan knew he'd be clear of the front door's camera angle if he waited for her at the rear door adjacent to the store's parking lot. The camera over the back dumpster appeared out of order, no sign of blinking lights or an active lens, and it was angled in a downward trajectory, offering little security except from dumpster-diving rats and racoons.

Since Serena had posted her photo in her meetup profile, it was easy to spot his willing victim as she crossed the street to meet him, her long dark hair bouncing with life as she scurried in between traffic. He had never posted a photo of himself and she had never asked.

Serena was a lot pudgier than her photo let on. *One empanada too many*, he thought. Her clothes clung to her rotund frame like Sanmartino's sculpture of The Veiled Christ in

Fractured

Naples. Donovan remembered the haunting image from a church trip to Italy and it stuck with him for the past thirty years, how the sculptor had captured the serenity and the beauty, almost a sensuality, in death.

Shaking hands and sharing smiles, they entered the donut shop through its parking lot entrance and sat at the first table close to the door. It was near the bathrooms and away from the crowd by the cash register.

"Don't think I'm crazy," explaining more than apologizing for wearing his hooded sweatshirt on such a sultry night. "I've been under the weather," as he coughed into his sleeve, taking off the midnight blue scarf he had tied around his neck, the one he would soon share with her. Soon, very soon.

"Of course, one can never be too careful." Serena agreed.

"No truer words were ever said," he smiled.

"Why don't I get you a cup of tea with honey," she offered and was on her way to place an order before he could refuse. Donovan was happy that she was so giving. It meant he didn't have to face anyone at the counter and could slink into his corner chair.

She returned placing the two cups on the table before heading to the bathroom. It gave him just enough time to spike her drink with some of his old stash of Rohypnol, assuring she'd play nice on the trip home, wherever she lived. He had taken them from the job years ago and hoped like hell they were still effective.

The two sat just long enough to finish their teas quickly, Donovan making sure no one made eye contact with him as they walked out the door. He played with his scarf, mindlessly weaving it around one hand and then the other, as if warming it up for its main act.

"Such a nice scarf," she said, admiring her ribbon of death, not knowing how soon she'd be wearing it.

He thanked her and then suggested they walk outside because he could use the fresh air, having been so sick and stale inside his apartment for the past few days.

As they stood to leave, Serena steadied herself by grabbing a corner of the table and collapsed into her chair.

"Are you okay?"

"I don't know, my legs suddenly feel wobbly. Maybe I'm getting that bug you have," she wondered. "It's been going around."

"Do you think you can make it to the rectory? My car is parked on the side street behind it." Donovan suggested he'd help her make the short walk across busy Gun Hill Road, knowing his intent was to pull her into the basement steps since he didn't own a car.

He grabbed her from under her elbow and steadied her around the waist. She was still a bit weak-kneed but walked fine enough. He had never seen a Roofie take effect so quickly and he was glad his old stash still held a kick. He knew he'd have to act quicker than planned. *I defiled her virginal body*, he laughed to himself.

Slowly they made it across the street, dodging yellow cabs and motorcycles, dancing in rhythm to the honking horns which they ignored. Donovan's adrenaline kicking in big time. *Stupid bitch, she's drawing attention to us like a beer-logged teen being dragged home after a long night breaking curfew.*

"I think you need to take a rest for a minute," he said, guiding her to the steps leading to the church's basement. The darkness of the night shielded them as did the cinder block wall which supported the steps. If he had to snuff her out here, he could do it, but he needed to make it quick. At least the floodlights over the parking lot were out. *They'd be on by now if they worked.*

Fractured

She sat quietly on the steps, suggesting, in barely a whisper, that it might be a good idea for him to bring his car here to get her. Mumbling her last utterance for help.

He placed the scarf gently around her neck, cradling her head into his shoulder. She was too weak to fight back. Too weak to realize she had brought this on herself. Too weak to see his actions were not caring and empathetic as he cradled her and then slowly placed the baby's pacifier in her mouth and his hands over her nose and mouth. She couldn't spit it out. He applied too much pressure for her to fight. She couldn't breathe, she was too weak. Too weak, much too weak, as she grabbed at the scarf which she'd admired just moments earlier. She scratched at her own throat to pull it off. She couldn't find his hands in her delirium. Too weak, too, too…and it was done.

He removed the scarf placing it in his pocket and gently slid her gold and amethyst ring from her right hand, taking a souvenir for his efforts. He left her lying like a sack of potatoes on the darkened steps.

Murderous death was anything but serene but at least tonight it was quiet!

Chapter Twenty-One

June 21st

Sirens ripped through Saturday morning in Williamsbridge as crowds gathered at the gates. Kids doing bike wheelies in the parking lot found Serena Gomez slumped on the church steps.

"One nudge and she toppled over," the kid told Detective Hank Summers. He knew enough from TV to be honest and let the cops know he moved the body...but just by accident.

"My friend screamed and cried like a little baby," his buddy gave his version to Detective Sergeant Lou Lopez.

"He was lucky to have you there," Lopez choked back a laugh as he complimented the kid's *mature* handling of the situation. "Smart thing you found the officer on the corner."

"Yeah, they're always there. Probably the safest corner in this 'hood," the kid said. He had street smarts beyond his years.

The detectives got a few more details from the kids before directing an officer to walk them home. No twelve-year-old should start their day finding a dead body. Heck, it was a bad way for anyone to start their day.

Fractured

"Breaking news, this morning, police say a woman was murdered on the church steps in Williamsbridge overnight. We go to our reporter Christine Shian on the scene. Chris…" The headline was a full-frontal assault as she turned on the TV. Her face cringed in frustration and anger as the reporter's voice recounted the events, recounted the children coming upon the body…then announced to the world, there was a baby's pacifier stuffed in her mouth. That secret couldn't stay secret for long, not with a pair of kids playing Dick Tracy.

"Damn fool," she screamed from a place so deep inside, from a place only she could visit, her past. "No one to save her. No one to protect the kids? When will it end?" Her frustration boiling over at Donovan and all the other men who ruined her life. She needed to fight back and she needed to win. He needed to be eliminated.

Tonight would be rushed, even for her. No one ever called her impetuous. No, she was methodical, quiet. She could've been a spy, seeing all, studying human behavior, understanding her place in the shadows before finally striking out.

It had been nearly a month since she took the life of the first Father, the one who mattered. She thought Donovan would disappear by now but the more she tried to ignore him, to snuff him out of her life, the stronger he became. Her own kills seemed to empower him.

She wasn't good at this. She was used to helping people. She spent her career doing just that. Taking a life was his game. But how many innocent people had to die before the final chapter was written?

Her single-minded bitterness made her unaware of the notches she had etched into the butcher block cutting board as she chopped onions for her two-egg omelet. She chopped and sliced a bit too hard as the blade cut its way into the birch wood, all but destroying the surface for the future.

Just below her façade, boiled a lifetime of hate, of anger, of abuse. She had been told to stay in her room one too many times as the groans and cries of adults leeched their way into her chamber. A steady stream of strange men violating her mother as she was forced to listen and told to keep quiet. Where was her Father then? Where was Donovan? She was left alone in a world she didn't understand with no one to protect her.

She had nothing to confess tonight. Regret didn't enter her psyche as she walked into church. It seemed no one else in the Bronx had any regrets either since the place was empty of all but the dust which gathered where few came to kneel in penitence or reverence.

She could hear Father Torres rise in his tiny confessional, grabbing for the doorknob. It was time to close up shop for sinners before the evening vigil started in another hour.

No worries, she'd be quick. The unknowing priest had barely time enough to look up as he entered the church aisle. She was waiting for him.

"Hello, confession is just ending, my dear."

"No need, Father. I have nothing to confess.

"You had one job to do, to protect your flock." She looked him in the eye, just inches separated their very breath from brushing past each other in the aisle.

Father Torres looked at her quizzically, never sensing the danger ahead.

Fractured

"I'm sorry, my child, I don't understand." The reverend asking for an explanation when there was none. It's hard to explain the need to kill to someone who's never done it.

"Forgive me Father, for you have sinned." A quick tug at Pearl's reliable trigger and Torres had his answer…a tug at his heart he would never remember and a bullet they would never find.

Eternal life grant unto him oh Lord and let perpetual light shine upon me.

Chapter Twenty-Two

"Looks like we've got ourselves a trifecta, eh, Tommy," Maggie walking up on her partner who seemed to always beat her to the scene. "How do you get here so fast?"

"Because I drive a 2010 SUV and not a 53-year-old car." He knew it would hit a nerve.

"Hey, I don't make fun of your kids."

"Please, take one of mine, I beg you. I've got five," he quipped back. "Warranty's up on all of them anyway.

"I'm so tired of this wack job getting me off the couch on a Saturday night."

"Ooh, and the boss doesn't look too happy either," Maggie observed as Assistant Chief Bradshaw hurried over to them. The faster he could turn it over to his detectives, the sooner he could get back to dealing with One PP. The Police Commissioner and the Mayor were both waiting to hear about the connection between last night's murder and the new hit on a Catholic priest. There's no such thing as coincidence in the Naked City, just eight-and-a-half million stories in a dark web of intrigue.

Fractured

"Flynn, Martin," Bradshaw greeted them with a lift of his chin.

"The vic is Father Torres. Pastor says he was just finishing confession for the day, getting ready for the evening vigil. Parishioners found him when they started showing up for the six o'clock service," Bradshaw gave them the rundown.

"Like Wojcick, he took one center mass but again it's a through and through, and again there's no bullet or casing." Bradshaw gave his detectives what little he knew himself. With any luck, maybe there'd be a bullet fragment inside the body but they'd have to wait for an autopsy for any more.

"Not good, not good, less than twenty-four hours after the last murder here." Martin shaking his head in disbelief. Maggie biting her tongue to say something about the Binky link.

"I've got Summers and Lopez back at the house already. I need you two to go over this place with a fine-tooth comb. I don't care if it means speaking to everyone whose windows face the church," Bradshaw's sharp directive was laced with frustration.

"That's a lot of windows, Boss." Martin could get away with sarcasm with the Chief. Maggie, not quite yet. "It's surrounded by apartment buildings and storefronts," he continued stating the obvious.

Tension built on the sidewalk as residents, already shaken by last night's church murder, started screaming for more police help. The red and blue lights, which flashed from patrol cars and assorted official vehicles, seemed to have the same effect as a strobe light on heart patients, spinning the crowd off balance, inciting them to explode. If the clergy weren't safe, then surely, they weren't either.

The foot soldiers on scene did their best to contain the two reporters who arrived, waving their microphones like police clubs, demanding answers for their story. Everyone in a rush to judge, everyone shouting for answers.

"Chief Bradshaw, Chief Bradshaw, have you linked last night's victim with Father Torres?"

"Were the two involved?" The crude query meant to generate a salacious headline for the Sunday papers did not fall on deaf ears. Bradshaw, Tommy and Maggie each heard it but chose to ignore it. To respond at this stage would be not only irresponsible but could get them into a heap of trouble if they bit off the head of the news hacks who masqueraded as true journalists. It was a lose-lose situation and the sooner they could put a lid on it the better.

"The Commissioner has already called in the FBI's Behavioral Analysis Unit. They'll be at headquarters at eight Monday morning." The Chief was frustrated the brass felt the need to call in the feds. He knew the District Attorney wouldn't like relinquishing control of this case either. The lack of confidence in their own police force stung like a slap in the face.

"Wrap up here and head back to meet with Summers and Lopez," Bradshaw continued instructing his detectives. "We've got a lot of work to do between now and Monday and I've got a news conference at eleven with the Commissioner and the Mayor downtown."

"Nothing else matters until this case is solved, ya hear me?" It seemed like a rhetorical question, but this wasn't the only case on their desk. Maggie and Tommy were already over-worked, like every other detective in the city. The NYPD had suffered a shortage of investigators since 9/11 and it only seemed to be getting worse. Yet the high-profile cases always got the attention they demanded.

Chapter Twenty-Three

"Hey ladies, looks like we're spending the night together," said Tommy as he came upon Summers and Lopez in the squad room.

"Where's your side kick, Super Girl?" Lopez asked taking a shot when he didn't see her bringing up the rear with two pizza boxes.

"I guess one of us stays hungry tonight." Maggie said, holding her own with the boys but doing all she could to restrain herself from lashing out.

"Can't you kids play nice?" Summers encouraged them.

The two teams inhaled the pepperoni and veggie pizzas as they stared at their white boards. For a while, the only sound among them was from the dying florescent light and the overhead ceiling fan which blew hot air around the room while teetering on total collapse from its precarious mount.

With their timelines now standing side by side, the vics laid bare before them, the four detectives realized the feeding frenzy the two killers were enjoying.

"We've gotta imagine the first kill at Tolentine, Father Richard McNamara, triggered this whole deadly chain," Tommy hypothesized taking the lead. "But why him? Why

McNamara? And how does the Clergy Killer know the Binky Killer from the past?"

It was a shared hypothesis among them that Binky came out of retirement after fifteen years on golden pond just after McNamara was gunned down. It couldn't be a copycat who was killing the women now because the pacifier clue was held close inside the NYPD years ago. No one outside those working on the case knew about that signature mark. Those cops were either retired now or gone, only their kids, like Maggie, left to recall the gruesome detail.

"Clearly that key fact never made its way to the press or they would've tied the string of cases from fifteen years ago to last night's killing when they reported the story," Maggie said. She knew that would've been the hard lead if the media recalled today the serial killer from yesterday.

"So, Binky comes out of retirement after McNamara was killed," Summers said as he slid over a third white board to their crime-fighting pow-wow. This new board would allow them to connect the dots, visually mapping dates, times, places, trying to see a joint pattern between the homicides.

"Something about that McNamara hit got under his skin," Lopez wondered, staring straight ahead at a whole lot of nothing before them. Some detectives thought better in a rapid exchange of ideas while others took silent pauses to reflect and plot and find some clarity in the evidence. Then again, the obvious lack of evidence here could be a dead-end.

No one knew these cases better than the detectives working on them in the moment. They lived and breathed the facts and evidence and literally walked in the shoes of the victims from the time they sipped their first coffee until the time they crawled back home, too exhausted to think any further.

"We need to delve further back, look into what made Binky tick years ago. What was his trigger?" Summers still not realizing that Maggie was aching to dig into the cold case files her father had locked in a box when he left the force.

"Would you guys mind if I looked through the Binky cold case files tomorrow?" Maggie asking permission to cross the territorial lines. "It was my Dad's case. I may see and understand something that might not be obvious to you guys," she directed the query to Summers and Lopez. Tommy sat back, glad to see she was playing by the clubhouse rules and understanding how much restraint she was exercising.

"Knock yourself out, Flynn," Lopez readily agreed to let the rookie detective work the weekend while he relaxed with his kids. "We're a team, right? Maybe your Dad will speak to you. God knows, we need someone to point the way."

Chapter Twenty-Four

June 18th

*C**ranky, hot, exhausted, what a way to start the day.* Maggie didn't get much sleep after getting home from the brainstorming session at three in the morning. The Sunday Times and Daily News she had grabbed from the newsstand just under the El on Westchester Avenue still sat on the kitchen table where she had tossed them last night before falling into bed. She didn't mind living outside the city so long as she could be near the beach and her Mamaroneck condo was just a five-minute walk from the shore. It allowed a serene escape from the insanity and grit of life in the Big Apple.

"Death at God's Door" was the catchy front-page lead dreamed up by some rim man at the News.

She knew the headlines hadn't changed overnight. She'd be one of the first to get the call had anyone else been killed.

She also knew the media wanted answers and the city had the right to know. If only it were that easy. Why are people outraged when the police don't solve a crime quickly? It's not like the killer, any killer, is waving a white flag of surrender downtown at One PP.

And why do those same people scream even louder if there is a quick arrest, protesting there was a rush to judgment in arresting yet another black kid? Why would anyone want to be a cop these days? They're damned if they do and damned even louder if they don't.

For Maggie the need to do good, to help the victims was imprinted on her Irish DNA. Her ancestors had started the NYPD in the 19th Century when New York was a dangerous place. A lawless society is a deadly society with people existing in a bloodbath of chaos. Anthropologists would argue we've come a long way since the club-bashing, knife-wielding days of the 1800s, while left-leaning liberals would say New York corruption has barely evolved from the days of Tammany Hall.

The body of the story that followed the spurious headline was built largely on speculation. In these days of hot tips from Twitter and readers thinking the Onion and Snopes offer real news, journalism had become a joke, a one-liner written by people who didn't know how to delve below the surface of a press release. Heaven forbid they did their own investigation to get to the truth. Joseph Pulitzer and Ed Murrow were certainly spinning in their graves.

Maggie wasn't surprised at the conjecture in black and white. The papers had column inches to fill and people calling for real answers weren't going to find it in an atmosphere of fake news.

Chapter Twenty-Five

The thud at the screen door jolted her out of her morning routine of feeding Cuddles his breakfast before showering and getting dressed. No church for her this Sunday morning, or any morning, ever again. She had little faith in the word of God when he seemed to walk right out the door all those years ago, as she watched…over…and over…and over again, despite the cries of "Oh God" from her Mom which never seemed to be answered.

She looked out the window onto the porch and realized the paper boy's pitch had improved greatly since she reprimanded him for always missing the porch by a mile. The big Sunday newspaper was in one of those red plastic bags to keep it from getting wet. The clouds had released themselves, covering the hot pavement with an early morning spritz before stopping. She was glad she could just reach the newspaper this dreary morning without leaving her little cocoon.

She hadn't felt him creep in behind her until faced with his squawk as she closed the front door.

"Not going to church this morning, dear?" Donovan's gruff reproach was an assault on her very being. There was no peace when he was around and the ongoing battle was wearing her down. "I hear the priests will miss you at Mass," he chortled.

In the past, she had refused to reply, thinking he would stop, would go away, would leave her life if she didn't respond. *Mommy always told me to keep quiet.* The silent treatment got her nowhere back then but she had finally found her voice.

"Your days are numbered," she hissed like an angry cat. Her growl causing the lines of her face to wrinkle and her broad gums to show. Even Cuddles hid under the table at the change in her tone as her anger and frustration filled the space around them. "They're going to catch you this time and when they do, oh, when they do, hell will seem like paradise."

He laughed heartily at her rebuff. "You always thought you were smarter than me, sitting in the corner, being so quiet, not letting them know you saw and heard it all on the other side of the wall," Donovan was revving up. A lifetime of tension releasing itself in a long overdue confrontation between them.

"I know what you're trying to do, to get me caught. You couldn't leave well enough alone, you stupid...dumb...bitch." His anger and hate exploded. Once released, its flow was endless.

"Don't you realize that it's always been me, always in control, eluding the very people you thought were your friends, your co-workers," Donovan sneered, his voice deep, gravelly, like unfiltered cigarettes singed by Jack Daniels. He was on a roll. His loud bark bellowed through the house.

He suffered the headaches but she felt as if her head would explode. She inhaled deeply, gathering strength, while he began choking on the dust and cat dander flying around the room as the tension stirred the air. It was filling the space, falling like an ash cloud after a volcanic eruption. It didn't bother her but aggravated his allergies to the point where his throat burned from the incessant coughing which choked his power into submission, a position that caused him great unease. She tried lashing out at him but her reach could not silence his verbal barrage. It was endless.

"They were my friends," she screamed emphatically. She came right back at him, no longer silent and saccharine. "You were the loner. No one was there to listen to you. People care about me."

"Don't kid yourself," he dismissed her with a sinister laugh from a place so deep it frightened her to her core.

Neither of them realized that just as their windows were opened to let in the spring air, so were those of their neighbors, who heard it all. The screaming which came out of nowhere. The man's voice when she lived alone. The push and pull of two people clearly at odds with each other. Who would win?

Her shaking was uncontrollable and then the tears started to flow. The dam burst, her wall of emotions finally shattered in his presence.

He watched as she played with the butcher knife on the table. One hand tugging at her hair, the other fingering the knife as she debated moving it straight toward his heart.

"You wouldn't dare, you spineless whimp." He egged her on.

She was swearing and breathing hard, muttering acrid nothings only she could hear. He was amused and shaking his head in disbelief that this whimpering pile of tears and fears could share his DNA.

How could they be from the same blood? How could they have lived the same life? Existing inside the dark and the light at the same time?

"Are you finished?" He asked, laughing as he did.

Hardly. She thought of how to make her next move.

His hand now over the knife. She was breathless, frozen as she had always been under his control. Does she run? She was empowered, or so she thought, but her feet seemed glued to the floor.

Where do they go from here? How would it end? Donovan rested the edge of the blade against her other wrist, holding her down like a shackle.

Him or me, him or me, him or me? The refrain teetered on the edge of her lips but muffled lest he hear her indecision. Her vacillation to yield would reopen the door to his reign.

She could taste the blood on her tongue. Cutting herself, her own teeth tearing at the flesh inside her bottom lip as she struggled internally to plot her course. She felt stronger but he was more powerful, undeniably. Then it happened.

He dropped his hold as quickly as he had grabbed it from her and was gone, out of the house. She didn't move. She was drained, exhausted, spent of ill-fated emotions. She dropped to the floor in a fetal position, just lying there in a puddle of sweat and tears until she fell asleep.

He thought she still had a lot to learn. She knew his biggest lesson was just ahead.

Chapter Twenty-Six

With the open road ahead of her, Maggie headed down the West Side Highway at dawn. Of course, driving down the F.D.R. on the east side to One PP would have been faster, easier but she never took the easy road. She usually took the most scenic path to anything. The sun rising over lower Manhattan, casting a positive glow on the city, refreshing it with a morning shower of light. The sunbeams bouncing off the less than pristine Hudson River looked like an open road straight to heaven. She couldn't be the only New Yorker who saw the Spirit Tower standing like a sentinel at the city's edge, reflecting on all that had changed since 9/11. Sometimes, you can't help but remember the past to realize how you arrived at the present.

Driving for her, in the absence of traffic, was cathartic, scrubbing away the ghosts of her father's case so she could focus on her own search for present day killers. Yet history always weaves a path to the future, revealing lessons which could help if applied correctly.

She pulled into a garage at the corner of Gold and Spruce Streets. It was the same garage where her Dad had parked this very car. It was still staffed by Jose who used to pull on her ponytail when she came downtown on weekends with her Dad.

"Miss Maggie, good morning. You're here so early today. Don't you know it's Sunday?" Jose opened her car door with a broad smile and missing a few teeth. "You're just like your Dad, always working."

She took it as a compliment even though he meant it as a kindhearted warning for her to enjoy life more.

"Crime doesn't keep holy the Sabbath, Jose."

"Ain't that the truth." He couldn't argue with the facts of life in a big city. You just learn to go with the flow, as sad as it seemed sometimes.

He waved at her with a reassuring promise to watch over her car.

Her polarized grey shades shielded her eyes from the bright light of the morning that confronted her as she ascended from the garage. You see things much differently in the daylight and in the silence around you when the work week fracas is missing. This congested little area of the city is quiet on the weekends, nearly dead. The only people out and about this early on a Sunday morning were other cops milling about One Police Plaza.

Most old case files had been digitized, where possible, but hard evidence, clothing, weapons, police notebooks, seized drugs, things like that, were held seemingly in perpetuity in cold cases. You see, there's no statute of limitations on murder. You keep hunting until the bad guy is caught.

Maggie had spent many days reviewing cold case files in the basement records room while she was a student a John Jay. Of course, she had limited access, as a student, but the old records clerk, Emma Kelly, gave her special attention and help with her research. Now, she could simply swipe her way into the records room with her key card, although the face who greeted her behind the inner cage was not whom she expected.

"Good morning, Detective Margaret Flynn," she said, identifying herself to the young man behind the screened area. She rarely used her given name since most in the department knew her as Maggie. They exchanged introductions as she signed in the log book. Still old school in the digital age.

Is this kid old enough to shave? She wondered as she smiled at the millennial guarding the treasure trove of evidence boxes like a guard at Buckingham Palace, barely cracking a smile and so serious.

"Good morning, Detective," he said, sitting a bit taller and firmer in his chair.

"You must be new, I don't believe we've met," she said extending her hand to greet the rookie. Maggie had to put this kid at ease before he popped a button on his starched uniform shirt.

He explained that he had been there just about two months and they now rotated working weekend shifts in the department.

Maggie inquired about Emma and was surprised to learn that she had retired just about the time this kid started on the job.

"I need to see case number 905-2001. It'll probably be a few boxes," she told the kid and asked if she could spread out the paperwork on a back table. She remembered the two conference sized tables they had amid the stacks of shelves which took up most of the subterranean level of Headquarters. It kept files from walking off and gave detectives a place to review without the need to haul off boxes and boxes of files.

"Wow," was the kid's first reaction. "Computer says it's ten boxes."

Fractured

"No worries, I've got all day." This used to be her day off but not recently, not when one of the city's most troublesome serial murder cases lands in your lap.

He led the way to the conference table and started bringing her two boxes at a time. A pair on the table, some on a wheeled cart and the rest stacked on the floor next to her.

She needed to be methodical or the day's task would be overwhelming. File number 905-2001 had been assigned as an umbrella control number to all six cases once they realized that all the killings had been orchestrated by the same perp. Each box was labeled with a sub case number, A through F, and the victim's name and contained all the evidence gathered in that particular murder investigation. Each box held a baby pacifier and all the gathered elements of a life snuffed out in an instant.

She didn't need to look at things like clothing and photos. She didn't even need to look at the medical examiner's report. Each one of them had been suffocated, smothered out of existence. She needed to review the notes of her Dad and Uncle Bobby. What did they see just after each kill? Their impressions, their theories, in real time, from fifteen years ago.

Maggie's head was spinning in only three hours. Six women lost their lives at the hands of a monster who's apparently still on the loose. What made him stop all at once? If she solves that, then maybe she'll understand why he woke up again this spring.

All the killings took place between September 30, 2001 and June 30, 2002. She remembered it was a time of uncertainty and fear for so many New Yorkers. The events of 9/11 had shattered their protected lives, the elitist invincibility that many Americans held dear ceased to exist that early September morning.

Did 9/11 rock his world to such a degree that he lashed out by killing innocent women? It didn't make sense to Maggie but murder is never logical to anyone but the killer.

If 9/11 was his trigger, what made him stop after six victims and nine months later?

The city's police force was stretched to its breaking point during that time. Resources were depleted and cutbacks were essential in local areas to find monies to train new terrorist crimefighters. Did something fall through the cracks here because of that?

Maggie started from the beginning, methodically delving in where the killer began, with victim number one, Case 905-2001-A. She opened the box which contained the life of Sarah Washington, the elements of her last seconds on this Earth squeezed into a cardboard file box. Is that the endgame of life? Do we all wind up in a box for others to review and discard?

Carefully, Maggie lifted the lid as if unleashing Pandora's dilemma, not knowing if she was waking a sleeping monster and releasing the source of great and unexpected troubles. Everything inside had been sealed into airtight plastic evidence bags, initialed by more than half a dozen people, making their mark each time the seal was opened with the hope of preserving the chain of evidence should this madman ever be caught and face justice.

She didn't have to dig too deep for her treasure. Just on top, she found a stack of skinny spiralbound notebooks held together by a crusty, brittle rubber-band, long since dried out and not worth the effort of holding the story together.

Despite the dark secrets locked inside, Maggie carefully held the stack in her hand, staring down as if finding a magic stone that granted wishes to the one who held it lovingly. For

Fractured

Maggie, her wish would be to step back in time, to be that teenager again, the one whose Dad taught her how to search for clues yet tried to shield her from life's dark realities at the same time.

He was organized. Each book was numbered. Each book bore the vic's full name and sub case number. They were written up near the top where the spiral wire binding wound its way half an inch past the dog-eared cardboard edge of the pad. Maggie remembered his habit of leafing the corner. He would thumb the edge of the pad repeatedly, over and over again, deep in thought, oblivious to his nervous habit, ignorant that his behavior had made the metal edge of each pad a spiral bound weapon to the next finger that grabbed it haphazardly.

She had absorbed more from watching him than she had ever realized until maybe this moment. Lost in her own thoughts, she wanted to call him, to ask him what made this killer wake up. Where had he been all these years? Did her Dad know the answers from where he sat now?

Help me, Dad. She found herself thinking of him, needing his guidance.

"*Quiet, church-going. Friendly, helpful.*" She smiled at her Dad's notes on the poor lady. There's something that takes your breath away, that literally hugs your heart when you see your parents' handwriting, long after they're gone. It's as if they've left a note for you to find just when you need it most.

"*Well-liked by neighbors...office clerk in mail room, in the shadows, not annoying.*"

"*Not too ambitious!!!*"

Maggie took notes of her own. She'd have to report back to the full team tomorrow, but this would take more than a day's inspection.

So much was swirling in Maggie's crowded brain that she gave herself periodic breaks. She'd walk to the corner restaurant to juice up on bad coffee with a splash of skim milk and half a sugar to make it palatable. Some cups needed the whole packet. The rookie police clerk at the front desk had his own supply of Coke to keep him revved for the rest of his shift.

She looked at the boredom etched on his face and knew this wasn't his dream job when he was at the police academy, presumably bright-eyed and bushy-tailed to catch bad guys. Instead, he sat behind a cage, watching other cops do the work he dreamed of while he logged them in and out, in and out, day after boring day, even if only in rotation. It was called paying your dues, something millennials often didn't understand.

Maggie placed her large coffee on the table, careful not to spill today into yesterday, as she pressed on with her research. The next notebook dropped from her hands and split open to the last page as it landed on the table crowded with papers.

"Maggie's Sweet 16…pick up cake and ring tonight"

It took her breath away. She'd be thirty-one tomorrow. *Thanks, Dad*, as she looked up to heaven, gently spinning her moonstone ring with her right thumb. Her Sweet 16 memento was a cherished reminder. Her Dad picked the moonstone because he taught her to always reach for the stars and keep her feet on the ground. She sipped her coffee to keep herself from losing it on the job and unleashing buckets of tears near the kid at the front desk.

Chapter Twenty-Seven

After eight laborious hours of sifting through evidence and reading the old files, Maggie was truly looking forward to her early birthday dinner with Uncle Bobby. Since he was in Yonkers and she was in lower Manhattan, they decided to rendezvous at the tiny joint they both loved on City Island.

There was little Sunday night traffic, at this time of year. It was too late on a Sunday to keep the kids at the beach on a school night and too early in the season, despite the early heat, for anyone to crowd the tiny shore community. She couldn't imagine trekking across the island bridge in bumper to bumper summer beach traffic. She remembered the smell of horses from the nearby stables in the summer heat just making the traffic jam that much less tolerable when she was a kid.

Tonight, with a cool breeze off the water, she was looking forward to sitting with Bobby on the back patio of The Black Whale. The old building with its wood plank floors and quirky nautical décor drew mostly a local crowd. Its menu was hit or miss but it was a great corner to grab a bite with friends and they never rushed you from a table to give it away to others.

Of course, Bobby was already there, sitting outside on the terrace at a corner table with a clear view of the door. So cop-like, so Italian as well, she laughed to herself.

"Happy Birthday, princess," he said lifting his mug of beer like an old pirate, comfortable in his own skin with no apologies to anyone.

"Thanks," Maggie said as they exchanged a warm embrace. "Dad sent me a birthday sign this morning while I was working at One PP." She explained the scribbled reminder in the dropped notebook and Bobby recalled her Sweet 16 as if it were yesterday.

"I know there must be a good reason why you're working a case that's not yours." His comment was more inquisitive than declaratory.

"You'd be proud of me," she smiled. "I've become a real team player." She explained the two teams had been ordered to join forces to brief the FBI who was expected tomorrow. She volunteered to review the cold case stacks because of her insight into her Dad's thought process and her access to her Godfather.

"What are you trying to prove?" He asked, knowing she was chasing shadows for approval.

"That I'm a good cop."

"So, do your own job and not someone else's."

"What are you my Dad's echo?" She snapped back with a cheesy grin. Her smile could melt hearts in an instant, making it difficult to scold her at all.

"Something like that."

She explained her theory to him as they snacked on deep-fried mozzarella sticks while waiting for their entrees. Death rarely got in the way of a cop's appetite.

"I think we've got two killers feeding off each other." She jumped right in. "They know each other. They know about Binky."

Fractured

"Do you think one is the original Binky Killer?" Stonestreet asked because he was unsure in his own mind. He wondered why a middle-aged man, who had seemingly settled into a quiet existence, suddenly came out of a safe retirement. Was it simply a rapacious appetite to kill? A hunger that had been satisfied long ago was suddenly ripe and ready again.

"I found your notebooks too," Maggie led him down her rabbit hole. "You thought it was a cop early on...by the third victim. Why?"

"There was a military precision to each kill." Bobby started explaining, started revisiting the case which continued to haunt him. There weren't many cases this big in his career and it was the only one that remained unsolved. He never liked leaving a job, or anything, unfinished.

"Each kill was clean, too clean, not a spec of trace evidence. That was the most troubling thing to the whole investigation because everyone messes up eventually.

"He used dollar store pacifiers to smother the vics and never left one fingerprint around their necks or anywhere else, not even on the pacifiers." He continued as it all came rushing back to him. "They never even had epithelials under their nails, except their own."

"We were chasing a ghost." He let the matter drop as the waiter placed his grilled salmon and her blackened tilapia down on the table.

"Could we just enjoy the evening now?" He asked, wanting to celebrate her life and not the deaths of the victims who haunted them long after the investigation went cold.

"I know. I need a break," Maggie agreed. "Sometimes I get carried away."

"Sometimes?"

"Very funny." Maggie could take a joke, even at her own expense. Life is too serious and most people forget that laughing is good for the soul.

The rest of the night went just that way.

"Do you remember when we went on that vacation with the rented camper?" She knew it was a trip neither of them could forget.

"Your Dad insisted that he knew how to drive that damn thing," Bobby shaking his head still in disbelief after twenty years. "He could never judge the height." The two of them now enjoying a roaring, heart-washing laugh.

"We pulled into that unmanned, self-serve gas station in the middle of nowhere Arizona and Dad nearly took the overhead awning with us when we left."

"Thank God, they didn't have security cams in the boonies...at least twenty years ago."

"It was so...I don't know...nice to see his handwriting today," she confessed to him, the only person she could fully open her heart to right now. "Sort of made me feel like Dad was still around leaving me notes in my lunchbox."

"I miss him too, kiddo." Bobby also shared his heart with the young woman he loved like a daughter. "Your Dad was a good cop and an even better friend."

Maggie's raw edge came from growing up the only child of a single Dad. Her Mom had died just after childbirth, so she never knew the soft touch of a mother's hand. Her Nonna tried but Maggie was definitely a Daddy's girl.

He was just one of those Dads, always present, always playful. The Dads who always protect and nurture their little girls but also teach them how to pitch in the big leagues. And Maggie Flynn was still swinging to show she could play with the big boys.

Fractured

"Well, you're like my Dad now and you've gotta love me no matter what," she smiled and batted her jade green eyes coyishly. "By the way, he loved you like a brother, you know," she reminded him as they got up to leave.

"Families, can't live with 'em, can't shoot 'em," he said, wrapping her in a big bear hug, telling her to drive carefully, knowing she could take care of herself but it was now his job to worry.

Chapter Twenty-Eight

It was only eight o'clock when Maggie put her key into the lock of her new condo. She took off her holster and secured her weapon in the locked drawer of her sofa table. This was her sanctuary. Guns didn't belong in paradise so she locked it away, out of sight but never out of mind.

She undressed and put on a Maroon 5 T-shirt, then plopped on the new, cozy microfiber couch. It was in teal, her favorite color. She was drained but only physically. She was glad to have Uncle Bobby in her life on so many levels but more than anything as a surrogate father.

People, especially thirty-something women seem to use birthdays to take inventory of their lives. Where am I going? When will I have babies? Why don't I have a boyfriend? There was never a right answer at the right time. Heck, most of the time there were no answers at all. The empty queries just resonated even louder in a chamber of isolation when there was no family and no friends to get you over the birthday slump. She had a handful of casual relationships, her close friend Karen from grade school and Mickey Malone who was always on the road, but her life was the job and her family was becoming the guys she worked with.

Fractured

Maggie should have been on top of the world at nearly thirty-one. A detective's shield. A job she loved. A brand-new home in a great Sound Shore neighborhood. And no one to answer to. Paradise, right?

She rarely succumbed to the single woman's angst but birthdays were meant to be celebrated with cakes and candles, booze and sex. Did that thought just really pop into her head?

The only slump she was in was a lack of carnal knowledge with anyone remotely attractive. She thought she needed to start drinking or get laid to clear her head.

Why do guys always say that? Does it actually work? The logic never made sense to most women under the same stress but she was happy to see that she still cared enough to laugh out loud.

"Maybe I should drink less and get laid more!

"Gee, wonder if I can order that up online.

"I doubt that talking to myself is part of the seduction." She was now laughing uncontrollably.

Too tired to sleep, she ran a steaming hot, lavender bubble bath, lit a lemongrass candle and made another wish. This one she would hold in her heart.

She popped open a new bottle of her favorite three-dollar Montepulciano from her preferred green grocer and decided to take "A Walk in the Clouds" with Keanu Reeves and Anthony Quinn.

The film was barely half over before she fell asleep under her cloud-like down comforter with the air conditioner set to sixty-seven degrees. She was meant to dream but she fell asleep with nothing but death on her mind. She expected another body would drop this week.

Chapter Twenty-Nine

June 19th

"Good morning," Tommy greeted an all but empty room as he walked in with a tray full of coffee and donuts.

"Where is everyone?" His partner was the only one in besides the Chief.

"They got the early morning memo. No one dead. No FBI till noon. You can sleep in," Maggie deadpanned in his direction.

"A man who listens," Maggie complimented his markings on the coffee cups which all looked the same except for the names on the lids.

"No, a man who's been trained by his wife," Tommy admitted with a recalcitrant pride.

"Yes, just one reason that I love Helen," Maggie giving him two thumbs up. Makes my job easier as your work wife."

They reorganized the squad room since the cleaning crew had rearranged things slightly trying to reach the dust and dirt which had piled up with three weeks of late nights. It made it hard for them to do their job. Now, everything looked spick-and-span for the feds due in after lunch today.

Fractured

One white board of the priest killings on the left. One white board of the church ladies on the right. And in the middle, a graph that looked like pie charts and arrows from a tenth-grade geometry class only this one had names, dates of death and nothing a tenth-grader should see.

The two worked the usual checkbox list of possible connections involving the Clergy Killer's victims. Schools, workplaces, friends, social media, doctors. They performed the usual post-mortem proctology exam of someone's life in search of a cure for death.

The only commonality was that they were all dead priests in the Bronx, probably all killed with a Glock 19 and all the crime scenes were spotless, oddly pristine. The striations on the bullet pulled from Father McNamara had confirmed it was shot from a Glock and they assume if it was one killer, he was using the same weapon time and time again.

The priests had little else in common. They had not studied or ever worked together. They each went to different seminaries spread out across the country and across the globe. So, how was the killer picking his victims? Why did he choose these three men in a city full of padres? Where did he get his training to kill with precision and leave no trace behind?

The first victim, Father McNamara, was a native son. Born and bred in New York. A graduate of Mount Saint Michael Academy, who studied at Saint Joseph's Seminary in Yonkers. Other than a short assignment in St. Louis, McNamara spent his entire pastoral career serving the five boroughs of New York City. At seventy-five-years-old, he was looking forward to retirement. His colleague said he did his job in a perfunctory manner, no longer able to give emotionally to those in need. Yet was that enough to kill for? Unlikely.

119

Next, there was Father Wojcick. A sixty-year-old Midwesterner who was well-liked in the Big Apple. He had been at Saint Barnabas for about eight years when he was snuffed out in the basement.

"Tommy, check it out, the first church lady, Dottie O'Neal. I think she lived three blocks from the Saint Barnabas rectory," Maggie said in a caffeine-fueled frenzy. "Go check the address of the second church lady," she ordered him over to the white board on the right.

"Yes ma'am," he hollered back and shouted the address and date of death in response, as Maggie scribbled notes in a chart on the center board.

The third clergy victim, Father Torres came from Ecuador only two years earlier. He was clearly well-liked by the parish's Hispanic community, organizing all the neighborhood Quinceñeras. Tommy checked his date of death against that of the second church lady victim, Serena Gomez, and the pieces fell into place.

"I knew it, I knew it," Maggie said, practically doing a happy dance.

When they were done charting commonalities among the three priests and the two church ladies, they stepped back to admire their own work. It all laid out perfectly in their new timeline.

There were two killers and it seemed one was fueling the other. They had guessed that last week but when they put it together, in black and white, it all made perfect sense.

"What do we have here?" Summers asked as he stepped into the squad room.

"Did you solve the case without us?" Lopez chimed in quickly.

Fractured

"No, but we did do the heavy lifting while you girls slept in this morning," Maggie giving back what she got without batting an eye. Her eyes weren't green with envy. How could they be when she was full of confidence?

The four detectives hovered together, around the center white board, like coaches mulling over their next move.

"The two are feeding off each other, like we thought," Maggie took the lead, explaining her outlined handiwork.

"He's going after women who disappoint him for some warped reason, while she's going after father figures, literally & figuratively."

"The McNamara murder seems to come out of nowhere but then a pattern develops," Tommy continued. "With each lady that's killed, a priest in the *same* parish is murdered shortly afterwards. So, it looks like our Binky copycat, if it is a copycat, is fueling our Clergy Killer."

They agreed it was time to tell the boss and walked in almost lockstep toward his door.

The three men innately deferred to Maggie, allowing her a seat in the only chair in the room besides the one occupied by Bradshaw sitting behind his creaky wooden desk. They also allowed her the courtesy of laying it out there for the Chief.

When she was done, Bradshaw inhaled deeply, slid back in his wheeled chair toward the wall, affording him extra support, and rubbed his shaved head like a Lucky Eight Ball while letting out a sigh. He took it in with the pause of experience, digesting it before making any rash assessments.

"Wait till the Commissioner and the Mayor find out that we have dueling serial killers." He knew he was in for one hot summer no matter the outcome. He explained this might change the FBI's game plan but it was critical enough that

121

Maggie needed to outline it for the feds before their briefing this afternoon.

Bradshaw encouraged his detectives to keep working their respective cases as a team and then routinely meet at the end of each shift to compare notes. They knew they had a lot of ground to cover and working together was the only way to tackle it. Right now, there's more competition between the two killers than between the detectives out to get them.

Chapter Thirty

It was the start of week five and with three dead priests and two dead church ladies, they still had no clear leads on a suspect in either case. They wore their frustration like a grey uniform, cloaking them in a Gordian's Knot of dead ends.

With tension mounting in the house and at One PP, it was about to get worse as a trio of FBI profilers came upon them, donning team jackets like they were the backline of the crimefighters here to save the day. Bradshaw noticed them through his glass wall. He jumped up immediately, lest any of his crew make an offhanded remark by way of introductions.

After a brief chat at the top of the stairs, he brought them in to meet his team, his front line of detectives, the ones really doing the dirty work to clean up the mess left by two serial killers crisscrossing a trail of death across the Bronx.

Bradshaw looked like the principal at a school dance trying to force kids from both sides of the city to meet in the middle. It wasn't going to happen, not here, not now. Yet each side made the effort, shaking hands and getting to work.

Maggie confidently moved to the front of the room at the Chief's invitation. She explained to the special agents their working theory that the two killers are shadowing each other with the Binky copycat likely fueling the Clergy Killer. She was brief, to the point, impressing most with how articulate she was in front of a room of seasoned officers.

The trio of feds looked, listened and then jumped in without deferring to the locals. Why should they? They were the FBI's Behavioral Analysis Unit. The BAU. They were The Profilers.

"These unsubs have some police or military training," said Special Agent in Charge Aaron Halsey. He was in charge of his detectives just like Bradshaw, but unlike the Chief, he didn't seem to have a warm bone in his body. Unlike Bradshaw, Special Agent in Charge Halsey carried himself with a superior air. He clearly believed that he was the smartest one in the room, even among his other *special* agents. He would call the unknown suspects what they were, unsubs in fed parlance, not killers or suspects like the amateurs in the local department.

"Any lack of trace evidence tells us they know how to cover their tracks well. Most unsubs mess up at some point but we seem to have two killers and five dead bodies without a bit of trace at any crime scene."

Maggie and Tommy, Summers and Lopez, even Bradshaw listened politely waiting for the profilers to tell them something they didn't know.

"They are intelligent and methodical." Special Agent Barlow Quinn jumped in to reveal their psychological profiles. "They plan each hit like an intricately choreographed dance between them. There's nothing random about how they're selecting these victims."

"Serial murder always has a monotonous psychological component to it," said the last of the fed triumvirate. Special Agent Sarah Sutton was the only one who reintroduced herself before addressing the team. "I know we're throwing a lot at you this afternoon but these killers have escalated out of control very quickly."

"They've blurred the line between a spree killer and a serial killer," Quinn offered his psychological assessment.

"A spree killer murders two or more people without a break, without a cooling-off period, while a serial killer is more methodical, developing a pattern with his kills over time," Quinn continued.

Quinn suggested the killers each have a pattern and their victims are not random but since they're in competition with each other, the murders are occurring more rapidly. Spree killer or serial killer? In this situation they seem to be one in the same and they're far more unpredictable.

Maggie appreciated the acknowledgement of the difficulties they faced and the explanation of who did what and how they were all working toward the same goal.

Halsey was tactical analysis. Quinn was obviously the psychological component. And Sutton, well, she was an expert on serial killers. That's a thing, a real thing.

Everyone in the room was trying to rationalize whether the current Binky Killer was a copycat or the original who's come out of retirement.

"Do they go to sleep?" Lopez asked. "And if they do, what would wake them again? What would make them start killing again?"

Serial killers all have triggers, when they first start and then again if they stop and restart. It's a logic that makes sense only to them.

"He'd be older now, probably in his mid-fifties. Would his age change his M-O?" Summers questioned who they were dealing with in the ongoing round-robin, trying to ascertain if they needed to make changes in their investigation methodology in order to catch him.

"Unlikely," said Sutton. "We agree that his trigger fifteen years ago was likely the events of 9/11. Now, it's something that reignited that fear of uncertainty. Maybe it was a relationship change. Maybe he lost his job. Something obviously took away his security blanket, his psychological safety net."

"He's older now. He won't take big risks," Quinn continued, as if from a memorized script, so precise was his profile. "He's organized. His methodology might change slightly but not his motivation."

The more the local detectives listened, the more they eased into the joint effort. These profilers did see life and death in a different way.

The Binky Killer is now trolling and hunting in a more confined geographic area and not citywide as fifteen years ago. Something is making him stay close to home.

"Maybe he retired. Maybe he moved," Quinn rattling the ongoing changes which anyone faces in their middle ages. "He's likely more sedentary now, not as adventurous as before."

Maggie and Tommy found the Binky analysis quite interesting but they needed to get back to the Clergy Killer.

"How is Binky tied to the priest killer?" Tommy jumped in to make the connection. "The pattern shows us they're reacting to or fueling each other."

"Maybe the Binky Killer restarted because he bragged to the second unsub," said Sutton. "They're probably about the same age. They're feeding off each other in a pissing contest.

"The Clergy Killer doesn't want to emulate Binky. He wants to surpass him, make his own murderous mark on history," Sutton continued explaining that dueling serial killers are rare. Most of them are loners with severe anti-social disorders.

Fractured

"The Clergy unsub is killing men who represent a father figure to him, quite literally." The profile volley was now back with Quinn. It was amazing how they bounced ideas back and forth. It was like detectives researching at the local level but this analysis was on steroids.

"Your psychological love map develops in childhood," Quinn revealed.

"Ooh, now we're getting juicy," Summers whispered to Maggie. "He had me at love map." She covered her mouth as if coughing to hide the smile under her hand. She couldn't help but smile because they had all reached their saturation point by now.

"How we develop and interact with our family maps how we deal with the world," Quinn continued. "If that wasn't properly established at the very beginning, then these killers will not have normal relationships. They'll have enormous trust issues with practically everyone.

"Both were likely abandoned as children in some respect, either physically or emotionally, maybe both. It left a huge imprint on their love map."

"So, all this craziness comes because daddy didn't play catch with them in the yard?" Tommy wondered if it could be that basic.

"That was probably just one symptom of the neglect but basically, yes.

"They become disconnected, cold, anti-social beings," Quinn affirmed the profile.

"Junior psychopaths on their way to serial murder?" Summers blurted out the sad reality that so many could face.

"There's no one for them to please but themselves. They don't care about hurting anyone because they believe no one cared about them," said Quinn. Sadly, he had too much information on this deadly stereotype.

"Does it run in families? Could we be looking at two brothers or a brother and sister?" Maggie wondered about the foundation of this fatally flawed love map.

"Possibly and they won't stop if that's the case." Sutton explained that the downward spiral had already progressed too rapidly.

"The kills are coming quickly, they're devolving at an unexpected rate because of this twisted symbiosis between them. The ultimate kill for one just might be the death of the other."

Chapter Thirty-One

The feds left with the promise to return tomorrow morning after digesting what info the crew had shared with them. They were also going to look over the Binky file from fifteen years ago, hoping to see something with a fresh set of eyes.

Maggie excused herself, saying she had to get something from her car but she needed to clear her head after the two-hour long verbal dissection of a pair of crazy killers. At that moment, Maggie was grateful that her love map appeared to be intact.

In the safe confines of her car she dialed and heard the phone ringing on the other end. She was glad she still had someone to call to share these great moments in her life. Moments of insight, moments of happiness, moments that required an *"Atta girl"* when the rest of the world often looked through and over her. Yes, her love map was intact and right now Uncle Bobby was her biggest cheerleader.

She proclaimed to him that her instincts were right and the two killers were feeding off each other. She couldn't see his big smile through the phone but she could hear it in his voice and she enjoyed the fatherly kudos which came her way.

"You and Dad always thought it was a cop," she reminded him as if he didn't think about it all the time, the worry that it could be someone he knew...someone who now worked with Maggie.

"If it was someone in the department, he'd likely be retired by now." He didn't reveal his real concern to her, the recognition that it could be somebody still on the job. Somebody watching her every move.

Bobby cautioned her to remain on her side of the fence and bring the clues in when the time was right and when all the players were in the room.

"So, how do we catch him?"

"He gets dumb or you get lucky," was his best guess. After all, if he knew how to catch the Binky Killer, he would've locked him up fifteen years ago. Now, this new deadly play-pal of his was a wrinkle in an already tangled plot twist.

"I'm proud of you, kid, now get back to work and have a Happy Birthday."

By the time Maggie returned to the squad room the guys had placed candles in a donut and began singing happy birthday. She was touched they even knew. After all, she hadn't been part of the team that long. Yet it was moments like these that gave cops the levity they needed to get through the slog of a normal day. Then it was right back to work and the ugliness of life and death.

Chapter Thirty-Two

June 20th

I t's always a good night when a body doesn't drop in the middle of a killing spree. That means the killers took a breather and the cops get a break, a chance to have dinner at home and sleep. Yet your body never catches up. Why do people always say that? Six hours of sleep can't make up for weeks of exhaustion. Do the math. Numbers don't lie.

The four detectives ambled in within minutes of each other, each of them looking like they were ridden hard and put away wet, which never sits well even with a work horse. Death will do that to you...even if you're still breathing.

Summers and Lopez had spent the day reviewing every aspect of the church ladies' lives. They put their habits under a microscope, everything from where they worked to what they did online, even their OB-GYN doctor. They put it all out there on the white board.

They explained to Maggie and Tommy that both church ladies did visit online meetup groups but stayed very local, keeping within the sphere of their home parish and there was no crossover among them. Their Internet surf and email history didn't reveal any mutual contacts and most seemed to be one-off connections with no established relationships. The ladies were basically loners, perfect targets for a deadly predator.

"You've gotta wonder that if it's the same killer from fifteen years ago, why has he narrowed his killing field to the Bronx?" Maggie asked what they had all been thinking. "I mean, if the Bronx is important to him, then why?

"Was he born here? Does he live here now?"

"If it's anyone with police or military training, they would know better than to hunt in their own backyard," Tommy said. "You would think, right?"

Their reluctance to share info on their respective cases had finally given way to a camaraderie to reach their end goal, to get these guys off the street and behind bars before anyone else falls victim.

"What connects these two killers? It may be evident only to them. It could be something so personal that it evades recognition by an outsider," Summers said. He had positioned himself on the corner of a desk facing the three boards. His collar unbuttoned, his tie hanging loosely, looking like he'd already done a day's work and it was only 8:30 in the morning. He stared blankly ahead while ideas crisscrossed in his mind.

"They're driven to kill by a shared hurt but each expressing it in different ways," Lopez said, agreeing with his partner. "It's as if they experienced that hurt together but differently, if that makes sense."

Tommy suggested that it may be a shared history of something so terrible that it was seen only by them and only their personal cat and mouse game can deal with it.

"Look at us, we sound like a bunch of special agent profilers," Maggie said, as they all laughed. They caught themselves, just in time, as the triumvirate of Halsey, Quinn and Sutton entered the squad room.

The feds were shocked to learn that the two church ladies had visited "female friendly" sites like Needle Nellies and Stitch and Bitch. A man would stick out on such sites, a woman could win their confidence easily. They explained that maybe they're looking for a woman and a man and not two men as they originally thought but there was no clear consensus among them.

"But no rapport was developed with any outsider, male or female," Summers said. "They each chatted only with members in the group or had an occasional one-off exchange with a newbie or an outsider."

The profilers understood the detectives' reluctance to see a link in the most innocuous of connections but when that's all you've got, it can't be ignored. The Binky unsub was preying on women in a virtual world with real deadly consequences.

"Women are not usually so physical in how they kill," Quinn said. He explained that's why he was standing by his initial profile that the Binky unsub was a man.

"Poison is usually a woman's weapon of choice," Sutton added.

"It's a reality that most women just don't have the physical strength to overpower their victims," Halsey continued. "It took a lot of backbone to gain physical control over someone like Dottie O'Neal. She didn't have a slight build and she was five-foot-nine-inches tall.

"The unsub was able to grab her from behind and smother her, seemingly without much of a struggle and all without leaving a bit of trace evidence.

"A woman of average build just couldn't do that." Halsey made it clear where he stood on the matter. It would take a formidable woman to strangle someone to death, even with the adrenalin surge of the moment.

"There's never any evidence of a struggle," he reminded the group. "That's why it's been so hard to initially determine the cause of death," he paused briefly as they all soaked in the data being shared. "More than half of all strangulation or smothering victims appear to have died of natural causes.

"If it wasn't for his signature baby pacifier at the scene, there's a chance we never would've found she'd been smothered.

"With no physical markings, no obvious fatal injury, no skin under the nails as if grabbing someone who's choking you, this killer was strong, methodical and quick." Halsey spoke confidently of his belief that the Binky Killer must be a man.

The four detectives knew that a good chokehold on a victim's carotid artery could mean lights out in as little as fifteen seconds. Add to that a hand over the nose and a pacifier stuffed in the mouth and death would be almost instantaneous.

Quinn went on to explain the differences between psychopaths and sociopaths. As a doctor, he clearly knew and understood the difference. But too often people used the terms interchangeably, often to their detriment because each could be a charmer in a social setting.

A psychopath acts more on impulse whereas a sociopath is more organized. A psychopath kills in the moment, violently. A sociopath plots out details.

A true psychopath doesn't have the neurological pathways to feel remorse. There's no moral compass for a psychopath. A sociopath, on the other hand, has a moral compass that is so skewed that deviating from the path of safe and acceptable behavior is normal for them. They act because they want to not because they need to.

"To put it as simple as possible, a psychopath is more violent and will often torture his victims for the sheer pleasure of it, enjoying the control and the impulsivity of the kill itself." Quinn tried to boil down the complexity of the illness to something as basic as black and white, night and day.

"For sociopaths, they are generally loners, they remove themselves from most situations and when they inject themselves into a relationship, they appear outwardly trustworthy but are conniving and deceitful to reach their goal which is anything but impulsive.

"Psychopaths are more likely to have a physical component in their brain chemistry or lesions on their brain.

"Sociopaths might have lesions as well, but their behavior is closely tied to their upbringing."

"There is something infantile about the Binky Killer," Sutton explained. "Just look at the baby pacifier he uses to choke each victim. There is no sexual component to these killings. In fact, he may be asexual. There is no release for him. He's killing to silence something from his childhood."

Maggie and Tommy reminded the group that the clergy victims didn't have an apparent connection except that each was killed shortly after a woman in his parish, apart from Father McNamara, the first victim.

"The revenge aspect of that plot sounds more like a woman," Quinn conceded. "She seems to kill a father who failed to protect his daughter, even if only figuratively."

But they were all experienced enough to know that the military precision of the priest's kill shots did not point to a female killer.

"Leave it to our first big case together to stump the profilers," Maggie leaned over to whisper to Tommy.

"We're dealing with two killers with a purpose and a plan that makes sense only to them, in a dialogue only they understand."

Chapter Thirty-Three

"You, stupid bitch. I can say that a hundred times but you never learn," Donovan chided her in a voice that grated on her like a tornado spinning uncontrollably in her direction. "You've learned nothing from me.

"Your sloppiness will get us caught. You don't just walk into a church and pop off a priest where anyone can catch you...unless that's been your plan all along."

"Who asked you here?" She snapped back, slamming the front door behind her, whacking the morning newspaper on the credenza.

"I've been just fine without you, quiet as a church mouse for years." She was angry, frustrated by his return. She didn't understand it. None of it made sense to her.

"That's funny, you, a church mouse," he chortled a snide laugh. "You're funny. Since when?" His ominous presence filled the space with a heaviness that made it hard to breathe in the still air, like a noxious gas, invisible to everyone but deadly to all.

She couldn't get rid of him. He was blood, poisonous, but blood all the same. Yet a lifetime enduring this verbal barrage had taken its toll on her mental stability and eradicated her already low self-esteem.

They knew each other's secrets, how to push each other's buttons, how to drive each other over the edge into their dark abyss. It's where their souls were buried in that dark corner in the back bedroom, the place where Mommy locked them in whenever she had company. Their view was the same, but their vision was not. You couldn't blink this hurt away. When she knelt in terrified religious obedience, he rose in fury, committed to erasing the waste from his life.

"Get out, just get out...out of my life." She tossed a cup at the wall as she yelled. Its chips rained down on Cuddles' bed. She always worried that the noise and her screams would have the neighbors calling police to her apartment, even though cops hated domestic violence calls because their hands were often tied by the victimized spouse, reluctant to press charges.

"You must be joking. It's my job to watch over you, you need me." He anchored himself by the door, now open and letting the sun shine into their dark little world. "I'll be back," he promised her and was gone in an instant.

She closed the door quickly, not wanting anyone on the outside to see the ugliness she locked in her secret space. It was tearing her apart. She needed to breathe freely in her own home. She couldn't take much more.

Do you know what it's like to wake each morning wondering if or when you might disappear? Whether today will be the day your life ends and his begins. She had struggled since childhood, isolated in her suffering, unable to reveal her secrets to anyone...as if anyone cared. She needed to have a life of her own without the darkness always lurking in his presence and the nagging voice in her head.

"He needs to disappear, to die would be better."

Chapter Thirty-Four

The death-watch clicked as they waited for a third innocent woman to be killed. It was inevitable. Death was coming. They could feel it in their bones and the double-team investigation meant they could tackle twice as much ground in less time.

Chief Bradshaw had greenlighted a consultation with Bobby Stonestreet, knowing full well that no one, not even the FBI profilers, understood the Binky Killer better than someone who spent much of his career hunting him down. So Maggie and Tommy no longer had to hide their discussions with him.

"If you're looking at cops, tread lightly," Bobby emphasized his warning with the pause and stern tone of his voice. "I mean it, you could be playing with fire." His Yonkers living room had become the satellite bureau for this investigation.

"If it's a cop, he's older. Maybe he just retired because he has more time on his hands to prowl," he guessed as much as they did. "It could be just one reason he started again after fifteen years."

Binky's victims, then and now, were all women who wouldn't be missed. They led isolated lives with little or no family to miss them and casual friends who never got too close.

"They're not adventurous or hookers, but women who rarely get noticed and who never say a word, even if they're stepped on or looked over," Bobby reaffirmed what the profilers outlined yesterday. Yet some things needed repeating. Sometimes it's the echo of a clue that doesn't make a sound until it lands in the perfect corner.

"He might think he's putting these infantile, socially immature women out of their misery."

"What about the Clergy Killer?" Tommy asked since it was the death of Father McNamara that launched this killing spree just over a month ago.

"Clearly, the guy's got daddy issues," Maggie quipped.

"My gut says it's a woman killing the priests, someone abandoned by her own father," Bobby said. He knew his opinion contradicted the feds from the start. People see what they want to see or what their experience tells them to see, but in real life the lines blur and all that matters is what can be proven.

"Women do use guns. Women can be great marksmen. Just look at Annie Oakley, fifteen and a champ," he continued.

"Do you see where I get it from?" Maggie deadpanned in Tommy's direction.

"The FBI profilers like to tie things up in a bow, in a neat little package," Bobby coached them. "But people are not neat and tidy. Life is sloppy…and murder, well, that's a bloody mess."

He reminded them, in his professorial way, that we all have good and evil within us, two halves, polar opposites in the same body. "They're probably both charming on the outside, wanting to befriend everyone, but it's their beastly doppelganger that we need to fear, that you seriously need to stop.

"One of them is leading and the other is following. Who's impressing whom? Who's teaching whom? Find that, find the killers."

Chapter Thirty-Five

Tomorrow was the summer solstice. Daylight was growing and his cloak of darkness was getting smaller, a reduced window of opportunity to kill undercover. Donovan had been doing this long enough. He knew not to take chances, not to snuff out the lights of someone where others could see.

He wondered why she was getting more coverage than him. Then he remembered. *It's that damn rule of three.* A trio of kills before they sit up and take notice. A trio of kills before the media gives you a cute little killer nickname. A trio of kills, that rule of three, to get the feds in on the action.

"Well, Miss Tonia Jones, three's my lucky number," he chuckled, not fearing his nemesis. She had gone into hiding after their morning confrontation. His darkness blanketed the house out in the open, sending her running for parts unknown. Without the risk of her mamby pamby caterwauling, he was king of the house.

He turned on his computer and found Tonia waiting in a private chat room. He had invited her in several days ago, a room he controlled, a virtual space which would disappear at the stroke of a button.

Fractured

Their virtual chats were benign at first. He told her his computer camera was broken but he was able to see her just fine! Tonia was atypical for a black woman in New York, which he found intriguing. She dressed as dowdy as a southern church mouse, donning a bulky floral top over what he imagined was a mid-length skirt. He couldn't see her full body from her laptop's narrow viewfinder but her pudgy face told him she was more than full-figured. Maybe that's why she didn't wear counterfeit designer clothing. What wannabe fashionistas couldn't afford they bought on street corners and in Chinatown, allowing every chick named Porsche and Tiffany to be blanketed in a fantasy. But not his Tonia...she was down to earth, a bit out of touch but down to earth all the same.

He knew she worked as a secretary, a title about as old-school as her wardrobe. What was left of her family was in the south. One of the Carolinas, North or South, who cared? He'd found her on the Singles in Wakefield meetup site, a red beacon for lonely-hearts seeking action. In this case, death was imminent and sex wasn't even an afterthought. He'd make sure that the only "*Oh God*" she cried out would be her dying breath.

He was charming but conniving. She was naïve and trusting. They were a perfect match, more than she knew. He invited her for coffee. Women felt safe with just coffee, as if merely sharing a hot beverage with a stranger was any safer than meeting them for a meal or a drink in a seedy, dark pub where even the roaches hide in the daylight. The cheaper the date, the easier the kill.

Without a moment's hesitation she offered her address, so he could pick her up. *Stupid, silly woman*, he thought. *So easy to please, even easier to smother. Why take her out when you can kill her at home?*

143

A public bus carried him across the East 238th Street Bridge. He didn't own a car, no registration to trace. He took public transportation, out in the open, no security cameras on these old buses.

He liked to people-watch and the bus was his classroom to study how they acted and reacted. Why were they on the bus? What led them there? Where were they going? Why didn't they have a car? Maybe they were outlaws, just like him.

The daily passengers saw the bus as a way to get to school or work but he saw it as a microcosm of humanity. The bus crowded with people, like a can of sardines, of people forced together into a quiet, desperate existence. He was merely along for the ride, the show. He wasn't one of them. How could he be? He was special, biding his time until he was back in the spotlight.

The green light winked in his direction as he crossed busy White Plains Road. He found hunting in his old neighborhood easy. He knew this area better than any other. It was easy for him to fit in, easy for him to navigate the hard corners and side alleys of this lower working-class community.

Tonia Jones lived just a block away from the El, on Furman Avenue. It was one of those old red brick, five-story apartment buildings that had weathered the changes of its surroundings for nearly a hundred years. As a kid, when Donovan was chased from his own apartment because his beautiful mother didn't want him around, he would pass this very corner on his way to trouble...or on his way to buy an Italian ice up on White Plains Road. Things were simpler then, at least for most kids.

Donovan's wretched childhood was ruined by women...by his Mom who never wanted him...by *her* who always drew more attention with her whining...and by all the nuns who never believed his stories about his Mom riding men like a pony while he was locked in the bedroom. Moans and groans, cries of passion not comprehendible by youthful ears. He could see them through the pinhole he poked in the closet. They were the images of a childhood that could never be erased, not even fifty years later.

This place was familiar to him as he approached the building. The glass front door was new but the tile in the lobby was still the same, hexagonal white tiles, now yellowed with time, with black tiles cracked and in an odd pattern meant to resemble a doormat. He could've gone real Bronx and pushed every button on the panel to gain access to the building but he pushed the only one that mattered at this moment. Tonia Jones in apartment 1K.

Great, right off the lobby for a quick getaway. He was always plotting his next move and the ultimate escape.

By the time he turned the hallway corner, under the stairs, she had opened the door and was waiting with the eager smile of a child on Christmas morning, all delirious and toothy. She was wider than he was tall and that's saying something. *Those laptop cameras should come with wide angle lenses*, he mused in silence.

"Hello, Sam, so nice to finally meet you." She extended her hand pulling him into her home as if she'd never let him go, a real, living, breathing man in her home paying attention to her. A real man with a fake name.

She offered to take his hoodie and baseball cap but he said he had a chill and was having a bad hair day. They both shared a giggle.

Instead of doilies, plants had taken over her tiny space. Big ones, tall ones, ones on chipped saucers, others blocking the window to freedom, still others hanging from hooks in the ceiling. Spider plants lived happily next to dieffenbachia. It looked like a bloody greenhouse and was just as humid as expected.

"You have quite a green thumb." He feigned admiration to charm his way past her initial nerves.

"Oh, it's just a hobby," she said coyly. "I wish I had a yard. Then I could really go wild."

He doubted she ever had a wild day in her life. *Poor thing.*

Of course, the dinette table was set for two. The yellow Lusterock table with its forged iron legs was clearly back to the future and right on trend for 1970. The dishes, also, were stylish when Scooby-Doo ruled Saturday mornings. This could've been his own childhood kitchen just around the corner.

"There's nothing better than the smell of perked coffee," he said as he eyed the aluminum eight-cup pot on the stove and the Chock Full o'Nuts can nearby on the counter.

"It sure is the heavenly coffee," he joked.

"Ain't that the truth," she agreed wholeheartedly as she brought the pot with an appropriate trivet to the table, lest she scorch its forty-year-old pristine top.

"I hope you like Apple Brown Betty," she said, turning away to prepare what snacks she had baked from scratch.

He didn't know what or who Betty was but she gave him just enough time to slip the Rohypnol into Tonia's coffee. So, at this moment, Donovan loved him some Betty. He was still surprised at the quick effect the so-called date rape drug had on Ms. Serena in the alley and she was half of Tonia's size, so he doubled the dose just in case her bulkiness kept it from kicking in quickly.

Donovan had stopped along the way in one of those side streets of East 238th Street. He knew a walk and a talk and a few bucks could get him some street drugs, quick enough, no questions asked.

Fractured

He didn't speak much about himself. He listened to Tonia. Women like men who listen, so why go through the exercise of making up a fictional version of himself when her story was so much easier and would end ever so quickly?

She explained how Tuesdays were her day off and that she only worked part-time for a local chiropractor. She had no pets. Her last parakeet died about six months ago and she couldn't bring herself to develop another close attachment so soon.

No friends, no pets, no family. He had two conversations running simultaneously, the one he half-listened to with Tonia and the soliloquy running her data in his own head. He fully participated in that one. He could multi-task easily.

Donovan waited for the elixir to take hold and complimented her baked goods. Women like that too, especially the genteel souls who devote their lives to house and home in hopes of a family. All too many feathered their nests never to have anyone come home to roost.

"Oh, my, it must be this heat wave," she said fanning herself with a lace-trimmed hankie she had conveniently pulled from its secure tuck into her blouse sleeve. "Maybe we should move back into the living room and get away from the stove."

Sure, that's it, the stove.

Tonia led the way as he followed behind cautiously. He needed to sneak up on her. She carefully sat in her favorite chair and invited him to sit beside her on the paisley-patterned sofa.

"Why don't you sit down and I'll be right back," he suggested. "May I use your bathroom?"

She pointed the way as her head rocked back. She snapped it to attention like a commuter aboard the evening train bobbing awake from the roar of her own snore, dripping spittle from the corner of her mouth.

147

She'd be out like a light, so he'd take his time, washing the dishes, cleaning up the kitchen. Tidying up his little mess just like Mommy always told him to do.

"Tonia, oh, Tonia," he called in a sing-songy manner to his dozing victim.

He slipped the Binky into her mouth, agape in its restful repose. Gingerly he placed his gloved hand over her nose and mouth and she continued to sleep…forever…no muss, no fuss, just the way he liked it.

Chapter Thirty-Six

June 21st

"First day of summer, let's head to the beach," Tommy joked as they headed north.

"If you mean Orchard Beach by way of Wakefield," Maggie said, sitting in the passenger seat of the squad car. They had learned about another dead woman overnight in Wakefield and figured the north Bronx neighborhood might hold some answers. As Summers and Lopez tried to track the Binky Killer, they'd look around for clues about the Clergy Killer.

"Just smell that ocean air. It's calling us," Tommy taunted her, his nose sniffing into the air like a dog smelling bacon.

"Smells like fried onions from the corner bodega." Maggie wanted to gag as the scent assaulted her nostrils so early in the day.

They had reviewed the white boards before heading out and prayed they'd find a link between all the vics, priests and women alike. Turns out Father McNamara was pastor at Saint Francis of Rome Church in the middle part of his career and Tonia Jones lived just around the corner.

Wakefield and Woodlawn were longtime Irish and Italian immigrant neighborhoods dating back to the Roaring Twenties. It was a long shot but they hoped that some old pub owner might remember McNamara from forty years ago. Even if the working-class men didn't go to church every Sunday, they knew the name of the local priest, always, just in case the devil got them into trouble and the Lord himself was needed to bail them out.

Most of the bars were closed this early in the day and many had changed their names and offerings from Irish music and sports nights to tamales and salsa Wednesdays.

"I always thought you were an uptown girl," Tommy teased Maggie as they walked the length of White Plains Road starting at East 233rd Street. Her knowledge of the neighborhood and its changes was proving helpful.

"Uptown Bronx, yeah," she said as she pulled him into the last Italian bakery sitting in the middle of the block just north of East 237th Street. "We used to get pizza shells in here all the time and crusty seeded "S" rolls.

"Now it's a café with tables and espresso, oh my." She paused as they entered the tiny Nonna's Café. She looked back and had to enlighten her partner once she saw the question mark on his face at the thought of a pizza shell. She explained it was the lazy nonna's way of making fresh pizza on a Friday night. The local bakery pressed the dough into pre-formed crusts and partially baked them so all that nonna had to do was add tomatoes, *mootz* and pepperoni for the perfect *a'pizza*. They agreed good police work was being part sleuth, part shrink and part serious foodie.

The morning rush had slowed so Gianni behind the bakery counter had time to chat with the detectives. His regulars sat closer to the kitchen in the rear of the store and

Fractured

Maggie and Tommy grabbed a table at the window after placing their order.

"Two cappuccinos and sfogliatelli coming right up," Gianni said, eager to please.

"On the house," he said placing the tray of tasty breakfast treats on their table. Hesitant at first, they demurred after he insisted that he was running a contest and they were the winners as the 100th customers of the day. He knew they were cops when they walked in the door but never revealed his early assessment until after their coffee and they introduced themselves.

Word of Tonia Jones' murder had spread fast. After all, she lived just around the corner and the *goombahs* who made a practice of knowing all and seeing nothing had a good handle on anything amiss in their little world.

Maggie and Tommy sipped and listened as the bakery gang and Gianni commiserated how the old neighborhood ain't what she used to be.

"The old-timers died off and my generation moved out," Gianni said, revealing his life behind the counter. "I grew up in this kitchen. Where was I gonna go?" He shrugged his shoulders and lifted his chin to the heavens as if he knew nothing else and his life's path was set in reluctant acceptance.

Gianni and his gang of neighborhood *goombahs* were a rough set in their sixties. Some bald, others badly needing a haircut and a good ear hair trim. Most of them had a chiseled exterior. Not chiseled like an Italian god borne at the hands of Michelangelo but sandblasted and weathered by Mother Nature. Their hands were big and rough. Old school laborers never primped with hand lotion like the men of today.

This was their corner of the world, all they knew and where they felt comfortable. They could just as easily tell you how many times the corner deli had changed ownership in forty years as how many times the Bronx Bombers had changed managers.

This was their social media, sharing the stories of their neighborhood without the need for cell phones, snapping chats or posting tweets. And good detectives knew that walking the beat and grabbing a coffee, face to face, was the only way to win old school trust.

After an hour, Maggie and Tommy heard more about Father McNamara in the bakery than all the questioning they had done in and around Tolentine Church weeks ago. This was their home and their kids were McNamara's altar boys in a past life.

"Back then, the media was so focused on church sex scandals, but they knew nuthin'," said a voice from the corner. "Tell 'em, Gianni. Tell the good detectives about good old Father Mac." The team shouted directions as if Gianni was their spokesman from his pulpit behind the food-stained marble counter.

"Ah, yeah, the good padre and his *goumada*," Gianni revealing the shocking secret as everyone shook their head in disappointment, everyone but Tommy.

"Get out of here," he said and then looked at his partner who was also nodding acknowledgement. "You knew this?" Tommy questioned Maggie in utter shock.

Maggie explained that priests with mistresses was more of an open secret in New York than the sex abuse scandals which seemed to come out of nowhere when that story first broke. "And they didn't just sleep around, they had families, like kids and everything, Tommy," she said. "Sorry to burst your religious bubble."

"Fuhgeddaboudit!" came an unidentified cry from the *goombahs'* corner table.

Fractured

Tommy's Irish Catholic sensibilities were shattered. They thanked the *goombahs* and decided to make their way to Barnes Avenue...the scene of McNamara's trysts...and where his *goumada's* old neighbor still lived.

Chapter Thirty-Seven

Tommy parked the car a block and a half away so they could canvas the area on foot while approaching the old grey shingled house. But a cop is a cop from a hundred yards away and all eyes followed them as they passed down the street.

"4364, 4368," Maggie read the house numbers, looking door to door until they came upon 4372.

"That's gotta be him," she said to Tommy. She knew the type. It was already eighty degrees in the shade this first day of summer but Signore Milleocchi was sitting on his front porch in a starched white shirt. His red suspenders holding up his tailored and cuffed pants, the red color to ward off the *malocchio,* the evil eye, which lurked nearby...or so he thought...pure Sicilian, through and through.

This was the porch where he grew old. The front yard was the place where he planted his roots in a four-foot square patch of the greenest lawn this side of fertile Mount Etna. This was the pulpit where he saw everything and nothing at the same time as the unofficial *padrone*, the Godfather, of this entire stretch of Barnes Avenue.

Fractured

"Buongiorno, detectives," he greeted them, barely peeking over the top of his newspaper. He already knew they were coming. Maggie could see three cell phones right next to his empty espresso cup sitting on the pedestal brass and green glass ashtray, a DuMaurier cigarette hanging precipitously by two inches' worth of an ash trail.

They don't make 'em like that anymore. She thought to herself. She knew his ilk was a dying breed.

"*Buongiorno, Signore, come stai stamattina*?" Maggie also knew that speaking even a little Italian would open the door to a more relaxed conversation. So, she asked him how he felt this morning and he invited them right up into his world.

"It's a terrible thing, a terrible thing, all this killing...and of the priests," he said shaking his head in disappointment. In his eighty-five years he had never seen such troubled times. "What's this world coming to when they kill a priest inside a church?"

"You want ah coffee? *Due minuti.*" His invitation was more of a polite command in a thick Sicilian accent carried over from his childhood long ago. They felt like they were already drowning in a sea of caffeine, after their morning visit to the bakery, but they knew it was impolite to decline an espresso, especially when told it'll take just two minutes. And as sure as city asphalt melts in a summer heat wave, Signore Milleocchi returned to the porch in two minutes with the largest old-fashioned Moka pot this side of Palermo.

"Father McNamara was always at the house next door, uh datta one 'dere," he directed them with a lift of his chin because pointing drew too much attention.

"I think, his *goumada*, she was an Irish girl, uh. Helen? Mary? I forget, you know how it is," he feigned dementia when it was convenient. That's how you play with the cops. Keep them guessing.

155

At first Milleocchi, and everyone else on the block, thought McNamara was doing a good deed, helping a single mother after one of her kids died. She had twins and he believed the little boy died from German Measles but he never remembered seeing the kid.

"Sweet-uh little girl-uh, she told me she was ah twin," he continued as Tommy took notes and Maggie tried to charm the old man into remembering what he conveniently forgot, names, conversations. She knew his memory was like a vault, holding a lifetime of secrets, unlocked only when necessary.

This was a man who prided himself on his little corner of the American Dream. His porch had been recently painted. His small patch of grass was routinely mowed and the winter cocoon had come off his fig tree two weeks ago, allowing spring blossoms to soon bear fruit.

"The priest, ah, he move away…then de woman, she make uh de money de old-fashioned way, you know," he continued, shaking his head in a disapproving manner. He was too much of a gentleman to detail the business of a local prostitute to a lady, even a detective lady.

Yes, Signore Milleocchi always saw more than he revealed, even when he didn't get a cut of the take.

Fractured

Chapter Thirty-Eight

"Get an old guy talking and they become a *chiacchierone*." Maggie now in the driver's seat of the old squad car. "This bomb has two-sixty air conditioning moving at twenty-five miles per hour," she complained of the ventilated breeze they were forced to rely on in a car with a leaky Freon line. Their routine had quickly become one of easy accommodation, easy sharing, easy revelations.

"A what?" Tommy asked about the Italian she easily slipped into, speaking casually, forgetting her partner's Irish roots.

"A *chiacchierone*. Keack-keyah-rohn-ay," she sounded it out for him, phonetically, emphasizing each syllable, like teaching a new word to a first-grader. "It means gossip in Italian." She loved educating people in her second language.

"I thought you were Irish, Maggie Flynn."

"You have a lot of misconceptions, Detective Sergeant Martin.

"My Mom was born in Palermo."

He could see this onion had yet to reveal her many layers.

They started playing their own game of Clue in the car, tossing the details given to them by Signore Milleocchi through an investigative sieve. Good detectives take it all in and strain out half of what they learn to get to the cold, hard facts.

Even if the old man's version of the story was founded in half-truths, they had to give credence to the idea that Father McNamara wasn't holier than thou.

Our Father, who art a daddy, blemished be they name.

"The kids were his," Maggie and Tommy blurted out the possibility simultaneously, laughing that they were already thinking the same, one team, one brain.

"The old man lost track of the priest after he left the parish? Yeah right!" Tommy knew this was clearly one of those half-truths.

Milleocchi had mentioned he thought the girl had grown up to work for the city, maybe even the police department but he wasn't sure. Maggie wondered if the NYPD's personnel records could be accessed to see if anyone in their fifties or sixties was a twin with a deceased sibling. Tommy advised her they could likely do so since it was the same department but they'd have to run it by the Chief to be sure.

He knew Chief Bradshaw would ask for a reason. So, what was their probable cause? That some old man thought a dead priest had an affair and fathered twins, one of whom might be a killer in the NYPD? They'd be laughed right out of the Chief's office with that farcical narrative.

"If my Dad and Uncle Bobby were right fifteen years ago, McNamara's kid could be the Binky Killer."

"Listen to yourself, Mags, a good cop doesn't jump over gaps in the facts just to connect the dots in a plot," Tommy had to rein in her enthusiasm before she was totally off the rails.

Their sleuthing volley questioned whether McNamara had fathered any children. They could search the state's Vital

Records department but they'd likely need a subpoena. Long gone are the days when Albany turned over vital records to anyone but proven heirs. They could also talk to Ray Peretti down at Saint Pat's but it's unlikely he knew, or would admit to knowing, any priests who planted their seed anywhere other than behind the pulpit.

"The cold case notes said it might be a cop but they were also pretty sure that Binky was a man because of the strength needed to smother someone to death.

"Your Dad wasn't certain it was a cop," Tommy reminded his animated partner. He kept an eye on her driving, noticing the more she talked details and theories of the case, the more adventurous her motion behind the wheel, darting in and out of traffic like a city cabbie trying to get to the airport at rush hour.

Their task was finding the Clergy Killer and not the Binky Killer who was trolling for women.

"Would a troubled young girl grow up to kill other lonely women? Unlikely," was Tommy's sage conclusion.

"True," Maggie agreed. "But she might grow up to kill daddy.

"So, you're saying that if there's a link between Binky and Father McNamara's sordid past then it must be a man?" Maggie questioned her partner's guess. "But as you keep reminding me, we're not out to find Binky, so let's stay focused on the Padre Killer, Clergy Killer, whatever the hell you want to call him.

"Maybe it was a jealous lover or the hooker's angry father or brother who shot him." Maggie was mumbling a litany of possible suspects like tossing spaghetti at a wall, hoping one strand would stick...soon...before another dead priest landed at his maker's altar.

"No way," Tommy insisted. "They'd be in their seventies, eighties, even nineties by now, not generally a stage in life when serial killers are born."

"Then maybe Father Mac's debauchery is something better left for God to deal with in the afterlife, while we figure out who cut him down here...because it's not just his life that was cut short.

"If Binky and the Clergy Killer are feeding off each other then they're probably about the same age." Tommy realized that two killers in their late fifties or early sixties made a lot more sense than a pair of greying octogenarians who killed in between Bingo games at the senior center.

Killing takes discipline. Killing takes mental tenacity. It takes a twisted type of fortitude. Killing takes time and that was running out.

Chapter Thirty-Nine

June 22nd

With Lopez and Summers pounding the pavement in Wakefield, trying to find a lead on who killed Tonia Jones, Maggie and Tommy headed to Westchester. It was not their turf and outside of their jurisdiction, but all they wanted was a face-to-face with the old department records clerk.

"I wonder why she never became a cop," Maggie said, as Tommy headed north on the Bronx River Parkway. "She really knew her stuff and how to find the nitty gritty." Maggie had called Emma prior to leaving the station to make sure she'd be home. Tommy barely remembered her. Working on cold cases was a rare thing indeed for most detectives in The Big Apple since they were overworked with their current caseloads.

"Not everyone likes to chase bad guys and play with guns," Tommy said, always quick to inject humor or sarcasm.

The rising sun hit Emma's front porch with a morning glow that warmed even the coldest façade. She was watering her hanging fuchsia plants, in full pink and purple bloom, as Maggie and Tommy pulled into a nearby parking spot.

"Good morning," she greeted them with the happiest of smiles. "It's such a gorgeous day. The smell of summer in the air," she said and smiled in their direction.

"It's been so long, *Detective* Flynn," she emphasized Maggie's new title. "Your Dad would be so proud of you."

"Emma, this is Detective Sergeant Tom Martin," Maggie offered up introductions between the old clerk and her new partner as they walked up the front steps.

They had gathered on the porch but the sole wicker rocking chair indicated Emma lived alone. No one stopped by to chat. Where would they sit? She was alone in a straitlaced, seemingly respectable life. Even her potted plants were lined precisely along the porch railing, not a dead brown leaf among them.

"I remember this young lady when she used to visit the records room with her Dad," Emma shook Tommy's hand with a firm grip. He was impressed at its strength. It told him a lot about the person. He never thought much of a lame, wet fish handshake. Such a person was generally insecure or so egocentric that they couldn't be bothered with social niceties. Yes, sleuthing was indeed part psychoanalysis.

"I don't know how I can help but I'll do my best," Emma said. Maggie's earlier call revealed why they wanted to speak to her and she did little to put off a visit from anyone. She said she had some fresh iced tea inside and asked Tommy to help by carry two folding chairs to the porch.

As Maggie and Emma spent time catching up in the kitchen, grabbing glasses and the pitcher, Tommy took a quick visual survey of the well-kept home. It was instinctual. He'd scan any place the first time he visited. Photos, furniture, magazines, all spoke volumes about the queen or king of the house.

Fractured

Emma's home had plenty of photos in tiny frames on nearly every wide surface. Pictures of her Mom, with her Mom, with her cat, all that mattered in her small world.

"Emma was key to computerizing records at One PP," Maggie bragged to Tommy of the older woman's accomplishments. She'd never do it for herself. Emma admired Maggie's spirited confidence and her energy to drive her career forward. She wished she had just a thimbleful when she was working.

Tommy thought it odd that the person who brought computers to the records' room still used an answering machine. He saw it sitting on a small table near the couch. No flashing lights meant no messages. It was a table topped with a large doily and the Yellow Pages phone directory on the shelf below. You can't get more old school than letting your fingers do the walking...and the talking.

"This lady could find anything," Maggie lauded the woman's talents as they all grabbed a seat on the porch.

"Oh, I never had direct access to the evidence," Emma quickly clarified, dismissing any notion of her importance. "I wasn't allowed to handle it to preserve the chain of evidence. I could only tell you which box it was in," she smiled demurely.

"Ah! But finding a trail of breadcrumbs is just as important as leaving them behind." Maggie's bon mots continued as if she was fan-girling over The New Kids on the Block.

"They rotate young rookie cops in your spot now. They don't have one clerk assigned to the records room just yet," Maggie said.

Emma explained that retirement takes some getting used to. You wake each day, for a few weeks, expecting to go to work. Realizing that's not an option, you then try to fill your day. "There's only so much knitting and embroidery one woman can do," she laughed.

"My family's long gone. I was an only child, so it's quiet right now."

Tommy was getting bored with this gab fest. Reminiscing holds little interest for someone who's outside the memory circle, like bringing a spouse to a high school reunion.

"Do you recall much about the killing spree back then?" Tommy asked, trying to move things along.

"It was a tense time in the department," Emma recalled. "Maggie's Dad and his partner, Bobby Stonestreet, they had a lot on their plate."

"I looked through the evidence last weekend," Maggie told her. "There's at least ten boxes and dozens of notebooks."

"What was the feeling at One PP? Did anyone have a clue about the suspect, I mean outside of Detectives Flynn and Stonestreet?" Again, Tommy pushing to see why Maggie thought this little coffee klatch would hold more value than a friendly sit-down between old acquaintances.

"I don't know what they thought," Emma answered, holding back what she had seen and heard. She was uncomfortable with Tommy's interrogation posturing. "You'd have to ask them. I just logged the officers in and out. That's all I ever did. Most of them just walked right by me.

"I'm sorry," she said, offering yet another in a lifetime of apologies, worried that they would learn the real truth if probing too much.

Tommy put a lid on the iced tea and biscuits session in under an hour and shook his head all the way down the freshly painted porch steps.

Chapter Forty

"Well, Detective, that was a whole lotta nuthin'." Tommy questioned his inexperienced partner as to why she thought that visit was a good idea.

"Sometimes women see things in a different light and she was always very obliging and helpful," Maggie said, defending her view. "I thought she might remember something that could've slipped by or seemed unimportant to my Dad and Bobby."

"I doubt anything slipped by your Dad or Stonestreet," Tommy reassured her.

"Too creepy in there. Too many doilies and dollies and dusty crap," Tommy amazed at how certain old women follow a pattern into the loneliness of their golden years.

"What happens to spinsters?" He asked Mags.

"And I should know this because?" She gave him a cockeyed look from the passenger seat. He had taken the keys from her after their lively drive to arrive...alive!

"Because you're a chick," he quickly replied. "It wasn't meant as a dig...although, if the shoe fits...I'm just sayin'!

"I mean are the dolls and dust ruffles always there or do they show up at the same time as the cats?" He was now laughing, uncontrollably, and his wit was not lost on Maggie.

"I think they show up at the same time as the mothballs and flannel shirts with frayed cuffs and pocket protectors."

"Ouch, the girl can swing."

Fractured

Chapter Forty-One

June 23rd

She opened the door and the muggy stillness in the air nearly suffocated her as she stepped toward her night's purpose. She couldn't worry about him tonight, where he was, what he was doing. Nothing would hold her back. Not the ashen clouds threatening overhead, the air heavy with regret. And certainly not Donovan. Soon he'd have no meaning, not in her life. She was focused on the task waiting for her across the East 238th Street Bridge.

As a child she wondered if happiness was on the west side of the span, a bridge she wasn't allowed to cross into Westchester. In the Bronx, she was locked in a world of sin without end, a world of abandonment and isolation, a world of yielding without escape. Tonight she was leaving her home on the west side, heading toward the darkness, back to her past, intent on redeeming her future...back into the dragon's den...across the bridge.

The threat of grey clouds, low on the horizon, indicated a storm was coming, long needed and much anticipated. She stepped cautiously toward her goal, walking slowly down McLean Avenue as it linked her yesterday and today. She had never been more determined...or more ready...as she waited for the light to cross the bridge. The walk would do her good, like prepping for a battle to get the juices flowing.

She reached the bridge to cross over just as the skies opened, releasing the tension in the air in a downpour that seemed endless. God showed no mercy once his wrath rained down. Yet nothing would hold her back, not even God himself.

She waited patiently for the storm to pass, under the red-striped awning of the corner pizza shop. Death was always in a hurry but tonight, she had nothing but time and hopped on the next bus to carry her across and out of the storm's path.

She thought about all that waited on the other side of the bridge. Just the thought of returning to her past made her skin prickle on this humid night. But she was compelled to stop him. No more innocent women needed to be hurt or needed to die.

Good cops were chasing his tail, wasting their time.

They want trace? I'll give them trace. I'll tie it up in a damn pink bow. She would end this fight where it all began, close to home. Then she'd pray...yes pray...like hell, that the devil inside would be gone forever.

Fractured

Chapter Forty-Two

A jumbo black golf umbrella shielded her as she walked from the bus stop the six short blocks to the Saint Francis of Rome Parish Center. Everyone looked the same in a storm, shielding themselves from the wind and the darkness of the blinding rain. The thud of the downpour pounded the top of the umbrella, making it difficult to hear the cacophony of traffic around her. Horns blaring. Puddles splashing. Everyone in a hurry to seek shelter tonight. No one drawing special attention until they collided with an unseen metal spoke from an oncoming umbrella, hitting, running, no acknowledgement of the invasion of anyone else's space.

The puddles pooled quickly in the deluge not allowing the storm drains to gulp down the overflow. The streetlights, which had come on during her short ten-minute bus ride, now lit a path on the dampened pavement like a landing strip guiding her way. She kept her head down with a focused determination as she followed the changing blobs of light and images, light and dark, life and death.

She wouldn't normally go out in wicked weather. It's not a night to walk around. But tonight, she had a job to do. The slight inconvenience of a thunderstorm wouldn't drown her determination. *This too shall pass*, she thought as she ventured forward.

With one hand on the umbrella, the other hand on Pearl tucked securely in her pocket, she was lost in thought as a passing car splashed her to attention. Looking up, she realized she'd already reached the corner of Furman Avenue. The yellow crime scene tape still evident on the building, now wet, shredded and pasted to the metal fence around the five-story walk-up where poor Tonia Jones had died three days earlier. Poor Tonia. All she wanted was a man to love her, to take care of her. That was all she wanted too…for a lifetime.

The late afternoon basketball game had ended about an hour before she came upon the Parish Center and she could see the lights were still on in the basement gym. Gym? That was laughable. It was more like a faux wood floor finished to resemble a basketball court. The Cardinal lived in his mansion on Madison Avenue while Catholic school kids suffered under the fiscal mismanagement that was limiting their exposure to a well-rounded education. That left Father Jose Rodriguez to be chief cook and bottle washer, pastor and coach and tonight the confessor would meet his maker. *Would redemption await in the afterlife?* She wondered.

She didn't want to kill again. That was Donovan's craving. She fought the urge to clean up his mess for years. Age brings wisdom or at least enlightenment. It was then that she realized she could only change her world. Everyone else had to fend for themselves. While she couldn't erase the past, she could at least alter the present with the hope of a better tomorrow…one without him. She knew they lived the same life but struggled with why they were so different. Killing was what she did…now…it wasn't who she was.

She expected the death of McNamara to silence Donovan permanently, to put an end to their dual torment. Instead, it

170

Fractured

resurrected his deadly instinct, made him bolder, stronger, forcing her to right his wrongs, again and again and again. Weariness wore on her like tight jeans with a vice-like grip, suffocating her under the weight just as Donovan squeezed the air...and the life...from each of his victims.

To change her world, she had to get rid of him.

She came upon the good padre in the basement. She was tired of wasting time. All this killing was exhausting, just like the mental gymnastics needed to follow Donovan's moves and then plot her own. It took all the leisure time out of her golden years.

Pastor Jose Rodriguez might have been a good egg. It didn't matter to her. He didn't do his job protecting his flock. He let Donovan get away with murder...again...and now he had to pay for his sins.

She was a good shot, always had been. Rodriguez never had time to turn around, to look his killer in the eye. *Pop, pop, pop.* Three shots in the back barely made a sound from the gun...or a whimper from the good padre. Silencers worked wonders, as did her aim. She didn't worry about bullets ricocheting in this vast space with its laminated floors. Normally she'd clean up the mess but not tonight.

Almost immediately, Rodriguez dropped to his knees and onto his stomach. It looked to her like death was instantaneous.

She shook off the damp, evening chill around the body, her raincoat splashing it as the priest probably had done many times before when giving last rites to the nearly departed. Instead of blessing the body with a liberal dollop of Holy Water, rain fell over him as if from the devil's cloak itself.

"Welcome him into paradise, oh Lord," she began saying the prayer for the dead as she'd been trained to do in her good Catholic home by her devout Christian mother. Suddenly, she stopped, frozen in place, taking in the silence, in a rare moment of shock. What had she done? Why does this keep happening? How can she make it all stop?

"Trace, trace, give them trace." Her initial whisper turned into a chanted mantra, over and over as she once again gave a purposeful shake of her whole being near the body, now lying face down at her feet. She knew that act alone would deposit all kinds of hair and fiber near and over the corpse. It would be up to investigators to find it.

She had always picked up after herself, always. To her, even death was orderly but not tonight. She wanted it messy. She needed it messy. She'd let the forensic guys clean up after her and lead them straight to Donovan's door. What else could she do? Point the proverbial finger and say, *"Here he is. Come and get him."*

She thought it odd that little blood seemed to be pooling under Rodriguez. Her inquisitive mind forced her to bend down and tilt the body to the side to look for exit wounds. She didn't waste much time. A quick tilt revealed no exit wounds, not one drop of blood from torn flesh, meaning he died instantly. Post-mortem lividity would have most of his blood pooling internally. And since the bullets, all three of them, were stuck in his body, she had little to take away…even if she wanted to clean up her mess.

She picked up the spent shell casings and placed them with Pearl back in her damp left pocket and realized she was still wearing gloves. Leaving fingerprints would be the big bow they needed on this forensic gift package. The evening rain mixed with sweaty palms made it difficult to peel the glove back from her right hand. She hesitated a moment about what to do with the stripped off glove. She couldn't get Pearl wet. She might still have work to do and she needed to protect her partner in crime as much as herself.

After placing the black leather glove in the right sleeve of her coat, she grabbed a basketball sitting center court. The padre's body blocked a shot from the top of the key. So, she grabbed the ball and easily made a two-point field goal. Yes, her aim was dead on!

Swish!   Yeah,   the   crowd   goes   wild,   nothing   but net…fingerprints…and a whole lot of trace DNA.

Chapter Forty-Three

June 24th

"Howdy do, partner," Maggie said as Tommy made his way through the ring of foot soldiers now surrounding the entire block. The Saint Francis of Rome Parish Center, the church and the old school were all cordoned off by a parade of cops as if they were there to honor a fallen brother.

The air was still in the heat of a spring morning. The rain overnight made everything bloom. Trees, especially the dogwoods, decorated the stark brick and shingle landscape. Yet, as vibrant as life was growing around them, the darkness of their day was on the horizon.

Tommy grunted. He was clearly not a morning person, especially on Saturday mornings. Their shift had always been nights for the short time they'd been together but this assault on the borough's Catholic priests had everything out of whack, including Tommy's internal clock.

He grabbed for a coffee cup in the cardboard tray knowing at least two of the coffees Maggie brought with her were meant for him. His brain couldn't function properly without a double dose of caffeine, each with three sugars, because if the coffee didn't give him a jolt then the sugar rush would surely do the trick.

"Father Jose Rodriguez was the Pastor here," she filled him in without asking too much of her seasoned partner. "He apparently was popped just after yesterday's basketball game.

"Doors were still open, people coming and going, parents picking up their kids, the list of suspects could be endless.

"Just look at this vast pool of Looky-Loos," Maggie said, her eyes canvassing the growing crowd across Barnes Avenue and down toward Nereid Avenue. The word was out. Another dead priest in the Bronx and Saturday morning shoppers were gathering like a fire sale at the dollar store.

Maggie and Tommy collected what little info the patrol officers managed to muster in the initial canvas of the block's residents and the church staff. The dead priests, the onlookers who saw everything but knew nothing, it was all becoming too routine. They needed a break.

They spied Summers and Lopez making their way under the wisps of semi-taut yellow crime scene tape. Their badges gave them access while the flimsy yellow barricade did little to keep death from God's door.

"Figured we should all be working this one together, sort of like the killers" Lopez quipped as Maggie and Tommy nodded in agreement. "Our last vic lived just around the corner on Furman."

"Yeah, their song and dance routine has now become a quickstep in lock step," Tommy acknowledged the escalation by the dueling killers, one killing quickly on the heels of the other. "Maybe if we stop one killer, we can stop them both," he said. The trick was finding their lair.

The four detectives donned their blue booties and snapped on blue nitrile gloves to keep from further contaminating an already busy crime scene inside the makeshift gym. Empty bags of chips crunched underfoot. Crushed paper cups and empty water bottles decorated the floor with straw wrappers strewn like confetti. Two worn basketballs, one nearly flat, begged for someone to pick them up and shoot some hoops. It was a tattered carpet of leftovers from last night's game.

"What a mess," Maggie mumbled to herself. They huddled around the body lying in the middle of the chaos.

"Another clean kill, detectives," the forensic examiner had beat them to the punch this morning. "No exit wounds either, so we should be able to pull the bullets at autopsy. Looks like three went in and none came out.

"It was a busy night," the examiner moaned. "We've got autopsies lining up downtown."

"That may be true, but you know the Mayor has made this a top priority," Tommy reminded him.

"Roger that," said the white-suited body-catcher, lifting Father Rodriguez to a waiting stretcher after the detectives got a quick look and any details they required. They didn't need to hover over the cleric too long since photos and trace had already been taken and collected.

All that remained of his passing was a chalky outline where children played just hours earlier.

Fractured

Chapter Forty-Four

June 26th

*K*ids *everywhere, the little rug rats,* Donovan thought to himself. It was the first Monday morning of summer vacation. *They'll be crowding the streets for the next two months until the school cycle starts all over again.*

They posed a big risk for him. It didn't get dark in the summer until almost nine o'clock. Kids saw everything and told anyone who would listen to them.

He remembered how they used to play stick ball and stoop ball just around the corner when they were told to get out of the house. Those hot summer days would last until it was too dark to see, too dark to know who was coming and going from their own home.

Go play in the street. What did that even mean? He heard so many Bronx parents say that to their kids that the kids themselves jumped the gun, often beating their parents to the punch. "I know, go play in the street," they would mumble when they saw that look of rising temper and frustration in their parents' eyes. All kids know that look. The one that means get out of here before you get a beating.

I know, go play in the street. He had said it to his Mom so many times that it became the song of summer...so many summers.

Donovan heard the music of the Mr. Softee truck in the distance. If "go play in the street" was the eternal lyric then certainly the Mr. Softee theme was the melody of his childhood. He knew from experience that it was a block away. It's nine in the morning. It's like spoon-feeding kids a sugar rush for the rest of the day. Yet the melodic tune had kids in every apartment building, in every house, screaming for freedom.

"Mahhhhm, it's Mr. Softee. It's Mr. Softeeeeee. Mahhhhm, hurry, I'm gonna miss him." The louder they screamed, the crazier their squirming antics and the faster their parents looked for their last three bucks just to get them out of the house.

He watched from the corner. Someone had placed a bench randomly next to the mailbox. That always happens when a local *padrone* thinks he owns the corner, marking his turf with furniture. Donovan figured it belonged to some old-timer on the block, someone who hadn't yet finished his first cup of coffee. Donovan dared not linger because a fracas for control of the bench was sure to happen eventually. The block's *padrone* just dared someone to take his throne, anyone. He lived for the challenge.

Donovan just wanted a corner and a bit of time to strategize without raising too much attention.

He already knew a lot about her. When she woke. When she ate. When she left. And the same for most of her neighbors. He had been canvassing the neighborhood for a few days. He even made a guest appearance last Saturday morning to watch the cops clean up the mess of his nemesis at the Saint Francis gym.

The tiny street offered some protection in this all-seeing world of social media and closed-circuit TV. There seemed to be no cameras on this block and that was a good thing. He had scoped the scene the other day just after visiting poor Tonia Jones. But there were plenty of windows with plenty of retired, unemployed and underemployed neighbors just hanging out, watching the world go by.

He felt confident. Half the game is looking the part and Donovan did. So, people trusted him. Today, his usual jeans and dark hoodie gave way to khakis and a well-pressed, button-down shirt, unbuttoned at the top. His tie hung loosely below the opened button lest it choke him. He couldn't stand that restrictive feeling. His bushy mop of smog grey hair was stuffed under an NYPD baseball cap. As if any real detective would wear one, especially on the job, let alone canvas a neighborhood without a partner in such a high-profile case.

For Donovan, all it took was a knock on the door and he was in!

"Good morning, ma'am, I'm Detective Sergeant Donovan," he said as he flashed a badge which he had picked up on Mott Street for three bucks. You can find almost anything in Chinatown with ready cash in your pocket. Cash is always king on the street and the dealer's memory disappears as soon as the deal's done.

"We're visiting the neighborhood, hoping to find information about the priest killings," he said, offering her a quick reason for the unscheduled knock. "If you've seen anything, even the smallest detail, it could help."

He seemed friendly enough…and official…so she invited the angel of death to cross her threshold.

"We want to make sure you're staying safe." He barely contained his laughter with a broad grin as he stepped carefully

Lisa Fantino

into her world. *Lure them in with a false sense of security. It gets them every time.*

She was younger than the others. Maybe 40-ish. He wasn't certain, but she looked better, dressed better and didn't have a damn cat lurking in any corner. He could breathe freely.

She introduced herself as Tiffany Paris and said she lived alone now that her brother had moved out after their mother died about two years ago. *Who cares? I have a job to do. Let's get on with it.* He had no time to waste.

She kept talking. She was one of those. Once a woman hits her comfort zone with someone, there's usually no closing the floodgates to chatter.

It was early in the morning and she seemed all dressed up with nowhere to go. She revealed she no longer had to work thanks to a handsome life insurance policy from her dearly departed mother. *Who gets that lucky?* Certainly not Donovan? He had to fight and claw his way for everything from very young. Unnoticed, unkempt, unmanaged and finally unleashed.

No wonder you look so smart with your little hoochie dressed up in Gucci and Pucci, he thought.

Tiffany Paris! What a name, he mused. *These weak women named after things they'll never have and places they'll never go.*

"Well, Ms. Paris, of course I'm certain you know to lock your doors and windows, especially at night, and don't open the door to strangers without proper I-D."

She acknowledged his directive and he stared at her in awe. *You fool, you just let me in! Stupid, silly woman!*

She invited him into her well-appointed but dated living room. The furniture was probably her Mom's. The orange velvet sofa dated from the 80s and looked more the shade of rusty iron showing its age. The floral pillows in bright sunflowers were clean but worn. Maybe Tiffany had replaced

180

them in the last thirty years, but he doubted it since her life looked frozen in time inside her cozy nest.

"They've been warning us at church and at the community center about taking precautions. Everyone seems to listen but nothing changes. You know, it's The Bronx." She shrugged matter-of-factly and smiled in his direction.

They shared a quick laugh as he took a seat and she walked to the kitchen to get him a coffee, black, just liked he liked it. There was an ease in her walk, an unsuspecting comfort in her own home, just as it should be.

His quick eye noticed that she didn't have many photos decorating her home. He spied just two on the old mantle. One with her mother and one with her mother and brother, he guessed. They were young...and happy...and shared that family harmony.

Tiffany returned with a proper tray, two cups of steaming hot coffee and a sugar bowl and creamer. He appreciated the attention to detail. China, not paper cups. Silver teaspoons, not plastic. Permanence in a disposable world. They all seemed to focus on the need to maintain a happy home, a concept as foreign to him as happiness itself.

"Oh, where are my manners?" She admonished herself. "I forgot the tray of cookies and napkins. Martha Stewart would not be happy." But Tiffany seemed happy, happy and clueless, unaware that her useful time for serving others was about to expire.

He was quick, fast enough to slip a roofie into her coffee. He made sure to leave the tainted cup on the tray and grabbed hold of his cup to drink to his own good health.

"Would you like a cookie?" She asked, offering him a tray of store-bought treats as she returned to the sofa, stopping just before taking a seat. "Sorry, but I wasn't expecting company."

He knew her polite apology would be the last thought to trouble her. *Stupid, whiny women. Always apologizing for things they can't control, things they won't control.*

Tiffany walked toward the window, casually lifting it, letting the outside in, the ivory lace curtains blowing in a casual elegance. She relaxed into her corner of the sofa. He could tell that was her spot. Her cellphone, reading glasses and the TV remote control were on that side table. So was a box of tissues. Women always have tissues at the ready.

He assured her there was no need for apologies. In fact, things were sailing along quite smoothly, both enjoying the coffee she had graciously prepared and the small talk to occupy their brief time together. He watched her from the side chair he had positioned himself in, holding a fake notebook in his lap to look the part of a dutiful detective.

"I can't, I can't, I can't breathe." Her shaky voice rose in panic as she coughed and pulled at her neck hoping to dislodge whatever held her back. Her coughing was frantic. The look of terror in her deep-set brown eyes made them pop like when you squeeze seaweed to watch its nodules burst.

"Relax, you'll be fine," Donovan said as he sat watching her.

"Help me...please...help me," Tiffany begged him, struggling to speak, realizing he wasn't there to protect and serve. He wasn't a cop but it was too late. She began to lose herself. It's not that she didn't want to fight to live, she just couldn't. The wind had been knocked out of her and she couldn't breathe, not deeply, not nearly enough to survive. She could feel herself losing consciousness, her eyes heavy with the drug-induced slumber.

Tiffany fought to get up but stumbled like a drunken sailor. She fought to reach for the phone, to scream for help but all she could see was him. The last image she would ever see would be her killer's face.

Slowly, Donovan rose to block any of her feeble attempts to call for help. She was gasping for air, so screaming was out of the question. She struggled desperately to grab the phone in a last-minute desperate attempt to survive, but he slid it just out of reach. He enjoyed watching her struggle for it, the look of extreme fear, the desperation and frustration of not being able to help herself. It empowered him to do what he was good at...to end their misery.

The process was taking a bit longer than usual. It had been a good twenty minutes already but he had nowhere to go and clearly neither did she. He watched her head bob in and out of consciousness. When he had had enough, he came up behind her and placed one hand on her head to steady it and the other over her nose and mouth to seal the deal quite literally. *Oops*, he almost forgot her Binky as he reached into his pocket for the pacifier. *There, give her something to suck on!*

She came to briefly and tried to grab his hand holding the pacifier firmly in her mouth. Her fingers slid off the smooth texture of his gloves. She tried to cry out but her voice was silent. She couldn't open her mouth. She was choking. Inside she was screaming but no one could hear. Her eyes said it all. She knew she was going to die. *But why? Why?*

"Oh dear, it's just your time to go," he said quite nonchalantly as if he could read the question in her eyes. He applied more pressure to silence her struggle. Again, she tried to grab for his hand but her own would not move. What had he done to her? She was fighting her way through, struggling to stay alive but it was not to be, no, not today. Tiffany Paris succumbed in the only place where she felt truly safe.

He gathered the cups and plates he had touched and placed them on the tray with her sugar and creamer. He grabbed her cup and all of the cookies and took them into the kitchen. Everything went into a small plastic grocery bag he had found under the sink. Some rat or alley cat raiding the trash would have a sweet treat tonight. He had no time to clean up and wash dishes. He was surprised to see a dish of cat food by the back door and figured a calico was probably hiding in plain sight, but he wanted no part of it. He wanted out of there before anyone came calling. He scanned the place for a final check, placed a spare cookie in his mouth and grabbed a souvenir.

No loose ends for Donovan. He peered out her kitchen window where it backed onto a rear driveway. Mature trees and a privacy fence blocked the neighbors from a clear shot of any action at Tiffany's place. It seemed quiet in her rear yard and he took advantage to go out the back door. It wasn't locked. Why draw attention to himself when he could make a quick escape?

Donovan stepped confidently into the sunlight. The warmth of the summer day was like Mother Nature's pat on the back for a job well done. He walked down to busy Nereid Avenue and danced his way across a steady stream of traffic to the other side of the street. The mostly quiet residential Byron Avenue was a straight-shot to a neighborhood of auto body shops and warehouses which backed onto the El rail yards. It would be a great place to toss his junk.

As he passed a day care center, he was delighted to see it was trash day. The neighbors' tattered bits and scraps of unpaid bills, mixed with shards of glass and rotten onions, were placed at the curb. Assorted boxes and trashcans lined both sides of the street waiting to be relieved of their contents, remnants of a desperate middle-class existence. By the time he reached the corner of East 239th Street, he was able to place the trash bag in one of three dented and partially filled aluminum garbage cans. No one the wiser. The evidence would be on its way to some over-polluted landfill before noon and he'd be on his way, back across the bridge to make his next move.

Chapter Forty-Five

June 27th

Four priests, four women, although the cops only knew about three of them. All dead without reason. As if murder was ever justified to anyone except the sociopath who kills! It's a twisted rationale seen only by the executioner and out-of-reach for the profilers trying to stop them.

"It's still hard to say who's leading who but at this rate they're keeping a neck-and-neck pace with a death toll piling high in a very short time," said Special Agent in Charge Halsey. He tried to answer the rapid-fire questions coming from Maggie, Tommy, Summers and Lopez. It wasn't in him to display weakness or frustration, much less exhaustion from the round-the-clock investigation.

"Does this guy always wear a suit and tie?" Lopez whispered to Tommy in the back of the room. "It's hotter than Hades in here. I'm chafing just looking at him."

Chief Bradshaw stood in the corner, close to his office door, leaning against it for support. He bore the weight of this case on his shoulders. The brass downtown, the Mayor, the Cardinal, all thinking crimefighters can wave a magic wand and with a quick arrest, erase the evil from the Naked City. Life doesn't work that way and Bradshaw had more than thirty-five years' worth of proof on his side.

The FBI stood by their original profile from two weeks ago. The killers had to be two men.

"Women just aren't competitive enough with each other or with another man," said Special Agent Quinn.

"Guess they haven't met our Maggie yet," Tommy said proudly, nudging her with his elbow. She could take it from him. He meant in the nicest way, proud to be her partner. She knew that part of playing with the boys was learning how the game was played and not trying to change the rules just because she was a woman. Not everything had to be about sex and gender in the 21st Century.

"It's not derogatory." Quinn felt the need to explain with two women present as key players on this joint team. "Testosterone is what pushes men to compete, to score, to go for the biggest victory," he continued. "It's chemistry." As with most men, everything had a reasonable explanation, the evidence speaks for itself.

"So, it is all about size," Maggie quipped and shared a gotcha moment with Special Agent Sarah Sutton. "Women tread lightly and the boys try to carry their big stick."

The laughter which erupted was just what they needed to break the thickness in the air that hovered over this investigation. The tension, the pressure often suffocated their ability to lead normal lives beyond the ugliness. But they knew better than most that beyond death, there was always life.

"We still believe they shared their stories with each other somewhere," Halsey said, trying to get the focus back where it belonged. He was the only one in the room to smirk rather than share in the gut-washing laughter. Maggie doubted Halsey ever escaped the stranglehold from his button-downed existence.

"They're not the type to share their past with a group," Quinn continued. "Their sharing would've been more one-on-one, only with each other...and possibly his victims as a lure."

"Maybe in a bar, or a chance meeting in a park."

"But that contradicts the Binky Killer's current M-O," said Lopez. "His hunting ground has been more social...at church groups."

"Not really," said Sutton. "Think about it. No one in any of the church groups has ever seen a stranger at the meetings, no matter where or when they occur.

"He's not being social. He's charming one woman at a time." That's what true sociopaths are good at. Their charm was deadly.

The unsuspecting women had absolutely nothing in common except their need to belong to a group. The key to unlocking this mystery didn't lie as much in the victimology as in the killers' psychological profile. That just may be more important than the who, what, when, where and how of their attacks. It was the why!

"He's going after weak woman who disappoint him," said Quinn.

"He's got big-time mommy issues," Lopez said from the back of the room. After an hour rehashing the profile, he needed to stretch his legs and grab another cup of coffee.

"Exactly," Sutton confirmed.

"Then the other killer must have major daddy issues, literally and figuratively," Tommy said, still holding onto the nagging instinct burning a bigger hole in his career-long ulcer that the Clergy Killer was a woman.

For now, they were hoping autopsy and toxicology reports from each of the victims might yield some traceable DNA. Maybe then they could scope out the killers in military or police department records or any one of several criminal databases, most of them under the umbrella of the National Crime Information Center. The NCIC was the lifeline of the FBI to assist local law enforcement across the country, a virtual repository of gun owners, sex offenders, illegal immigrants and gang members all at the push of a button.

Chapter Forty-Six

It was just before lunch by the time the FBI pow wow was over. Maggie and Tommy needed to drop some paperwork downtown at One PP for the Chief, so they decided to grab a bite at one of the many food carts around Foley Square.

Neither of them knew many of the suits at headquarters. It was a building full of strangers. Tommy hadn't worked downtown in more than a decade and Maggie was generally known to the old-timers as Detective Lieutenant Sean Flynn's kid.

As they stepped into the lobby, Tommy noticed Emma Kelly entering the building.

"Hey, isn't that what's her name?" He nudged Maggie and steered her toward the left door and the security line forming just inside.

"Emma," Maggie acknowledged her presence but was a bit surprised, nonetheless.

"Maybe she wants her old job back," he teased.

Emma was just as surprised to see them and quickly volunteered that she was meeting a friend for lunch and then going for target practice. They all wished each other a good day and went about their business but Maggie was troubled. Her face was a wrinkled map of concern.

"Target practice? Really?" Her face scrunched in disbelief.

"Doilies, dollies and guns, who knew?" Tommy joked as they headed down the front steps. The midday sun blinded them but Maggie's squint was more befuddled than her partner's as he reached into his shirt pocket for his Ray-Bans.

"Don't you think it's strange?" She asked him.

"What?"

"Emma. She always seemed so quiet, never really socialized."

"And *that's* the take away bothering you?" His eyebrows raised, his brow furrowed as the question left his lips.

"Not the fact that she's going to target practice?" Tommy could also multi-task. As they walked toward the "Gyros to Go" van on the corner, his mind was spinning the new fact pattern presented by the one-time records clerk. Why would a retired old lady clerk feel the need to shoot? It wasn't part of her job description in the past, so why now?

"Gotta love lamb on a stick in the dank heat of a summer day," he said before taking a huge bite out of his foil-wrapped meat sandwich. "It's the perfect meal. It comes in its own neat little pouch."

"Neat meat," he deadpanned but kept right on chewing.

"Do you know where that guy parks his truck?" Maggie wondered. As New York as she was to her core, she couldn't bring herself to eat somewhere where the mobile kitchen was likely parked at the horse stables on the west side of the city. She remembers her Dad refusing a pretzel because he didn't know where the vendor went to the bathroom during his shift. No running water to wash his hands after relieving himself. Nothing like street food in the Big Apple.

Tommy tuned her out, just as he did his wife most of the time. He continued wolfing down his Greek delicacy while Maggie ate vanilla yogurt. But food was just a diversion to fuel the churning in their minds. The thought of an old lady, without a badge, shooting a gun just didn't make sense.

Chapter Forty-Seven

"Time for our weekly kiss-the-ring, meet-and-greet uptown," Tommy said as they walked toward the car. They had nothing new to share with the city's chief Catholic cleric, so they knew what to expect. Tommy's old school upbringing had him fearing the anticipated castigation.

"Have you actually kissed his ring yet?" Maggie asked rhetorically.

"No, I'm scaaared," Tommy replied, his voice quivering falsely. "I think flames may shoot out of it or something. We're the bad kids on the block."

Maggie just shook her head and grabbed the keys out of his hand.

Summer rush hour seemed to start earlier and earlier as they sat in a real traffic mess where Canal meets Varick.

"Oh, young grasshopper, why did you not take the East Side?" Tommy asked in a mocked reverent tone as if speaking to a student from a lectern. He didn't like sitting in the co-pilot's seat. He much preferred driving and he obviously understood Manhattan traffic a lot better than Maggie.

"Technically, it's six of one, half dozen of the other since Saint Pat's is on Fifth Avenue which divides the east and west sides. So, we're both right," she said defending her decision despite the roadblock to their schedule.

"Have you always been this much of a wise-ass?" Tommy already knew the answer, as Maggie just smiled.

Finally, arriving uptown and running late as usual, they were forced to pull into the last remaining parking spot at the corner of West 50th Street and walk toward the majestic cathedral. The twin white spires gleamed in the afternoon sun as tourists and commuters crowded the steps in admiration of the results from the recent completed ten-year restoration. Most of them craned their necks to stare into the heavens where the towers seemed to be a straight line to the angels. Sinners, on the other hand, kept their heads down, looking not to trip over their own feet any further than their indiscretions had already carried them.

If the public was impressed by the restored one-hundred-forty-year-old building, they should get a peek inside the Cardinal's residence. The whole complex took up a square city block where Tommy and Maggie found themselves again having to answer to the big man as they rang the brass doorbell.

"Anyone home?" Tommy was incorrigible. But aren't all Catholic schoolboys?

"I've been here more in the last month than in my entire Catholic school career," he continued. The recognition was not lost on Maggie who felt pretty much the same. There was nothing routine about visiting the Cardinal's residence, no matter how many times you've been, but especially not about murder.

They both stood a bit straighter as they were ushered into the salon by the same young, well-suited woman who had previously greeted them. Ray Peretti entered from the opposite door at just about the same time as Cardinal Donohue.

Fractured

"Good morning, Detectives, how are my favorite crimefighters?" Donohue offered a big smile and a sturdy handshake to Maggie and Tommy. He anticipated better results than the two detectives were about to deliver.

"I don't know, Your Eminence," Tommy jumped right in. "Will you still feel that way when we tell you nothing's changed?"

"How can that be?

"I have priests who are running for the hills, putting in requests for retirement and transfers in droves.

"I have parishioners fleeing to churches in Westchester just for Sunday mass." Donohue was understandably frustrated but so were the detectives searching for a killer...or two.

"Priests don't want to hear confession in the Bronx. That's a problem for us," he admitted. He continued standing, clearly in control of the room, intimidating even if not intentionally.

"Our team and the FBI have been working non-stop for a month, but these killers are playing a good game, a very good game...with each other...and with us." Tommy defended the investigation which seemed at a stalemate.

It was hard to understand. There were no threats. Nothing odd in any of the churches. No notes delivered to shocked newsrooms looking to score big on the summer's hottest story. It wasn't playing out the way it should, the way it had when the Son of Sam went after young women in the late 1970s. He taunted the police with notes that played out in the press. He was typical, if serial killers can ever be typical.

These twisted criminals like to make their mark, like to get the attention they crave and believe they're entitled to for whatever warped reason fills their grey matter. Yet other than the dueling competition of the kills, these two unsubs were playing differently. They seemed to crave attention only from each other.

It was more of the same as Maggie and Tommy laid bare the lack of evidence and Cardinal Donohue listened reluctantly. Shared assurances by all to do their best. Shared promises that God was on their side. But not one of them offered a guarantee on prayer. How could they? Was God even listening?

The Cardinal abruptly called the get-together short and turned to leave for the next stop in his hectic schedule, as did Maggie and Tommy hoping to make a fast escape.

"Oh, Cardinal, I almost forgot, one more thing," Maggie called after him. She was going to take the heat on this query as she and Tommy had rehearsed before arriving.

"You were at the seminary with Father McNamara, correct?" She asked a question she already knew the answer to. Cardinal Donohue acknowledged their long history and friendship and wondered why she was asking at this late stage of the probe.

"Did you ever hear about Father McNamara having a family of his own, children, up in the Bronx?"

The Cardinal paused longer than usual for the usually expansive speaker. His eyes never leaving the subject of his wrath as he planned a reserved reply. Biting the inside of his cheek, tight-lipped and choking back his outrage at her impertinence.

"Detective Flynn, a Catholic school girl should know better than to ask such a question," he admonished her from his lofty perch. She felt the baritone voice of God speaking down at her from his six-foot-three-inch frame. "The answer is no," Donohue said as he stormed out of the room, followed by an unusually quiet Peretti shaking his head in disgust.

Fractured

"If we weren't already marked for a trip to hell, we both have a one-way ticket now, for sure," Tommy said. They walked quickly back to their car, dodging people along Madison Avenue and over to 50th Street in staccato rhythm. It was as if they were running, stepping lively to avoid any backlash emanating from God's front door.

He and Maggie knew what to expect but it had to be done. The question needed to be asked. If not now, then when? There was a whole lot more than just a tomb of sex scandals hiding in the church's vast collection of secrets.

Chapter Forty-Eight

June 28th

Hell comes in many forms. Early mornings. No sleep. Dead bodies on a hot summer day.

No one in New York was sleeping. They tossed and turned, wrapped in damp sheets which shrouded them in a heaping wet mess. The buzz of box fans and air conditioners was not a soothing lullaby. The uncomfortable heatwave suffocated the motivation to rise for work in the morning, especially when morning started in the middle of the night.

The neighbors near Tiffany Paris' home had enough. The routine summer scents of a New York City summer are anything but refreshing. Toss in a dead body, baking in the heat, and it's like living in hell. Summers and Lopez...Chief Bradshaw as well...had been called in during the sleepless wee hours of a scorching summer night to answer the desperate calls.

It was just shy of four in the morning and Barnes Avenue was as active as a block party in July. Bradshaw had beat his detectives to the scene by about ten minutes, just enough time to get the lowdown from patrol.

Fractured

"Whadda we got, Chief?" Summers asked as he and Lopez neared the boss.

"Neighbors called. They couldn't take the smell or the crying cat any more.

"Patrol called Fire to take the door and they all nearly keeled over when they entered." Bradshaw filled them in on the grisly scene.

"No one had seen the vic, Tiffany Paris, in two days and the cat had nothing to eat, you figure it out," he said with a lift of his chin and a disgusted shake of his head.

"M.E. just got here but one of the patrol officers says it looks like Binky strikes again. There was a chewed-up pacifier near the body.

"Brace yourselves. It's not going to be pretty in there," Bradshaw warned his men for the gruesome task ahead of them.

Firefighters and patrol officers were doing all they could to avoid going inside while still securing the scene. The horrendous smell even deterred the neighbors from crowding the area just shy of the yellow crime scene tape.

Summers and Lopez had seen a lot in their decades on the force but no amount of death from gunfire or stabbings prepares you for a rotting corpse. The old Vicks stick they kept in their pockets might help as they dabbed it under their nostrils, but they could smell her from the street and that wasn't good.

They donned blue paper booties and gloves and stepped into hell.

Lisa Fantino

What must have been an immaculate home was now desecrated at its core. What was left of Tiffany Paris lay in a pool of ugliness on the sofa, a bed of pillowed flowers now covered in death. Her cat sitting at her feet, undeterred by the activity around them.

Only the forensic photographer had followed the seasoned detectives inside. Even the pick-up crew from the M.E.'s office waited on the street for the greenlight to grab and go.

Hank Summers reached for his mouth, to shield it with a hand, to block the ugliness before them as he turned his back to recompose himself. His partner stared into space to avoid looking at the pile of bones and ooze on the couch. Everything which led to this point shocked the usually glib Lopez, leaving him speechless. The photographer moved through the scene on autopilot as if viewing ugliness through a lens made it less of a stark reality.

The three of them didn't have time to wallow for long, not with a killer racking up innocent victims like homeruns at the Stadium. They worked the scene together, stepping carefully, taking notes, measuring the space between life and death.

"It's strange, dontcha think?" Lopez asked Summers. "I mean she's obviously been dead awhile but there's no garbage around, no dishes in the sink. It's as if she literally stopped living the day she died." Lopez paused, realizing the paradox in his words. "If that even makes sense."

Yet in a strange way it did. You never know when you wake up in the morning if you'll go to sleep that night. You never know when you toss the trash if it'll be for the last time. You never know if the last face you see will be your killer's. You just never know!

Chapter Forty-Nine

June 29th

Thursday morning the fed profilers beat the team to the quick, already at headquarters, reviewing last night's discovery in Wakefield. If the two killers stayed true to their pattern, the feds thought this was a perfect time to lay a trap.

"Good morning, good morning," Halsey greeted Maggie first and then Tom, who were each surprised to see the FBI already at work.

"Good morning Agent, Chief," paying their respects to Halsey and Chief Bradshaw who started his day, again, before the sun came up.

"Commissioner had me call the BAU last night. The Mayor doesn't want another summer like with the Son of Sam in our city."

"Is our Mayor even old enough to remember Berkowitz?" Lopez asked, bringing his special ray of sunshine to the tired collective. They all smiled but knew instinctively that Lopez wasn't far off the mark. The Mayor was young, inexperienced and never had to deal with a serial spree of death from a pair of dueling killers. He thinks waving his baton will yield instant results.

"Why don't we take our seats and we'll get to work," Halsey invited them to gather for what had become a daily routine in a very short time.

The death tally now stood at four priests and four women. The cat-and-mouse game between the killers had leveled the score before, but now that the detectives and feds understood their pattern, it was time to lay a trap.

"We've seen these two unsubs dance long enough to predict their next steps," said Halsey. "Tiffany Paris was killed in her own home just days ago."

"She was a parishioner of Saint Anthony's Church, just blocks away," Special Agent Quinn reminded them. "Her death is going to irritate the Clergy Killer in a very short period. So, we'll have to act quickly."

The BAU team explained their desire to lay a trap. In the rhythmic, predictable dance of the two killers, there was now a priest at Saint Anthony's with a target on his collar. They would lie in wait and be ready to strike when death came knocking at God's door again.

Setting the trap would require some political finesse starting at the top and they would have to move with alacrity to beat the unsub at his own game. Maggie and Tommy were surely *personae non gratae* down at Saint Pat's but no trap was being laid without the full cooperation of the Archdiocese. Despite the trap being planned for the Clergy Killer, and it was their case, that request had to come from Assistant Chief Bradshaw. He was the boss and he could deflect the heat sure to come his way in a strategy planning conversation with Ray Peretti.

Fractured

"Ray, Ray, I'm truly sorry Maggie asked the tough question, but it had to be done," Bradshaw explained. He wasn't about to toss two of his best detectives under the bus merely because they were doing their job.

"Ray, death is ugly and it's our job to scrape down to the bare bone till we get some answers."

Peretti had devoted his life to the Catholic Church and knew many of the secrets which echoed through its hallways. Yet it was his job to keep them buried...in the catacombs...in the dark...never to see the light of day. He knew in his heart and soul that celibacy wasn't normal. How could it be if God created Adam and Eve to procreate? If all life and death began with God's creation and Jesus was the Son of God, then surely Jesus would follow his Father's path of enlightened creation and procreation.

"Ernie, one day, when this is all over, you and I will grab a single malt at McConaughey's Bar and debate the fact or fiction of priests with kids, but for now I'm doing my job as well. And it's my job to tell you that your guys truly pissed off the one guy who can greenlight your plot to end this."

Fifteen minutes and a callback later, Peretti told the Chief the plot to trap a killer had the blessing of the church.

Chapter Fifty

The plotting and strategizing session broke midday and Bradshaw suggested the team take a break. Go home. Grab a bite. He told them to do whatever they needed to reenergize and boost themselves for the very long night ahead.

"Let's take a ride to Wakefield," Maggie suggested as she and Tommy headed toward their squad car.

"Only if we can detour to Allerton Avenue for White Castle," he replied. Headquarters wasn't that far away and after all, it was lunch time.

"Chief said we needed to energize for the game ahead."

"I wish I had your metabolism," Maggie said, shaking her head as she looked over at her partner from the passenger seat.

"My wife is a lucky woman," Tommy replied, rubbing his belly like a baby Buddha. "She gets all of this."

"We might as well order a case. It's gonna be a long night." Maggie couldn't argue and suggested they make the burger pitstop after they visit the *padrone* of Wakefield.

Fractured

Maggie and Tommy agreed that digging further into Father McNamara's history, especially after the Cardinal's reaction to the question about possible kids, might yield better clues. They were hoping to find a path to a motive that launched this spree a month ago. McNamara had been a priest for more than forty years mainly in the Bronx. He also served in the parishes of two of the four victims. There's no such thing as coincidence except in the dictionary.

Chapter Fifty-One

Sure as the Yankees led the American league in a summer smackdown with the BoSox, Signore Milleocchi was sitting on his porch when Maggie and Tommy turned into Barnes Avenue and parked the car. His red suspenders were holding up suit pants over a well-pressed white shirt. The *padrone* was reading the daily Racing Form as the detectives walked in his direction.

"*Buongiorno*, detectives. *Come stai?*" The old man asked how they were doing just before peering over the top edge of the newspaper.

"I swear this guy has a spy drone in every direction," Tommy whispered as they walked, noting the old man's keen powers of observation.

Maggie made him stop along the way at Nonna's Bakery for a box of *babà* and *sfogliatelli*. Food always does the trick and it's safer than a payoff.

"*Bene, grazie, signore. E te?*" Maggie told the old man that she was fine in Italian and asked him how he was doing.

"You here about the lady killed last week?" Milleocchi asked, placing his morning cigar down on the heavy brass pedestal ashtray. He carefully flicked off the ash tip and blew it out so as not to waste it while chatting to the officers. Why waste a good hand-rolled Cuban cigar?

They explained that the murder of Tiffany Paris was part of it because the investigation was expanding. They needed to research the history of all the priests who were recently murdered. They were just wondering if anyone on the block remembered McNamara or the family he helped or where he went when he left.

"Signora Lenticchi," the old man said without hesitating. He directed them with a lift of his chin toward the house just to the left of his. The same semi-detached house where McNamara's *goumada* lived with her kids all those years ago. "*Normale,* she volunteers at the church in the mornings, *mah,* today *troppo caldo,* it's too hot. She's uh home!

"She sits inside with the air-condeesh her son bought her.

"*Mah, air condeesh, uhfa,*" he blinked his eyes and held the four fingers of his right hand to his thumb, waving them back and forth in a gesture of disgust and disbelief. "De air condeesh, it makes you sick when you're young...and when you're old! I sit here, with the breeze. I have uh God's air condeesh."

This guy never breaks a sweat, Tommy thought to himself as his young partner mesmerized the old man with her fluency in his mother tongue. He watched as Milleocchi quickly volunteered to phone ahead for them, so as not to worry Signora Lenticchi. He grabbed a phone from the trio of devices sitting on his small metal side table next to an empty espresso cup.

Maggie translated the old man's phone conversation for Tommy, explaining that old people in the old country didn't like cops. He commented that it wasn't much different anywhere these days. She said the old lady sounded like she hesitated but Milleocchi assured her they were there to help keep the neighborhood safe. So, she relented.

"*Ciao e grazie, Signore*," Maggie said, waving goodbye, Italian-style, and thanking the *padrone*.

"Yes, bye and thanks again." Tommy said, not wanting to feel left out. The old man smiled back knowing that Irish-American Detective Sergeant Tommy Martin would always be an outsider...at least to him.

"Tell me this guy's not still running numbers from that porch...with God's air condeesh and his Cuban cigars!" Tommy mocked him as they walked toward the house next door. Maybe it held more than a clue...maybe it held a motive for the original sin.

Chapter Fifty-Two

It was a short walk, literally just the other side of the driveway. They could see the Signora peeking through the vintage lace curtains of her picture window as they approached the front steps. By the time they reached the top, Signora Lenticchi had already opened the door.

"*Buongiorno, signora, con permesso,*" Maggie greeted the women in her own language and with respect asked permission to enter her home. She figured Signora Lenticchi and Milleocchi had been in this same spot for longer than she was alive. They were easily in their eighties.

"*Si, si, prego,*" Lenticchi said, inviting them across her threshold with a wave of her hand. She looked the part, dressed in an old pink *schmatta*, a smock, and wearing those sandals reserved for old ladies in the five and dime. They have a small wedge, just enough to make them feel sexy when they walk, and a single wide strap of gold vinyl to hold their foot in place lest they fall off. Vanity has no age limit but falling in place increases exponentially with age.

She invited them to sit down as she grabbed a seat in her recliner strategically positioned in front of her fifty-inch flat screen TV. Tommy imagined it was another gift from her son.

Lisa Fantino

He looked around and didn't know where to sit. Every upholstered and wooden surface was covered in lace doilies but he relented and followed Maggie to the sofa.

"My son, Angelo, he bought me dis uh bigga TV. He's a gooda boy," she said proudly, as if any Italian mother would ever criticize her son.

"'*Scusa*," she apologized, turning off her show. "Capri, my beautiful Capri. Dee best show on TV," she said. It was an Italian soap opera with the same drama as its American counterparts, only with better scenery.

"How can I help? I'm an old lady. I don't remember too much." She didn't really want to help but when Milleocchi asked, she couldn't refuse. They both still adhered to old school traditions, including neighbor helping neighbor and respect in the community.

Tommy was amused. She might be in her eighties, but like Milleocchi, there wasn't a thing that Signora Lenticchi didn't remember. He watched as Maggie asked her, in Italian, what she could tell them about Father McNamara. He didn't imagine there was much that she didn't hear between the common wall of the two semi-detached homes. They stood side by side, a mirror of each other, their secrets trapped between the plaster and lathe, nothing escaped them.

"McNamara, he disappeared when the church found out about his *amante*. *Come se dice*? How do you say? Lover," she said, shaking her head in an obvious sign of disgust.

"*Beh, putana*, no?" She asked rhetorically, fake-spitting to the side as if dispelling the very devil from her lips.

"You sleep with a priest? *Disgraziata!*" She was firm in her beliefs.

Tommy didn't know Italian but got the message loud and clear that this *signora* was not too happy with either McNamara or the woman she called a disgraceful prostitute.

Fractured

"But I stayed out of it. I mind uh my own uh business," she proclaimed. Tommy could feel his eyes rolling but was unable to stop himself. He knew she minded her own business and everyone else's on the block. Built-in security detail for when something went wrong.

Signora Lenticchi relaxed back into her chair, explaining that the church was disgraced. So, they banished McNamara to Staten Island. They removed him from temptation and allowed him to return to Tolentine's and the Bronx only after the *putana* had died.

She remembered a whole lot more when questioned for details on the children.

"Children? No children, only one little girl, dee poor thing." Signora Lenticchi said she always looked like a little ragamuffin, spending most of her time on the stoop outside while her mother entertained all kinds of men. They lost contact after the mother died. She didn't know where the young woman moved but heard she got a job with the city.

Signora Lenticchi could offer no more gossip from fifty or sixty years ago. Well, she probably could but she chose not to. She came forward into the present as if she was finished with the past, again tucking it into place in her feigned selective dementia.

After an hour down memory lane with Signora Lenticchi, Maggie and Tommy headed over to Allerton and grabbed a case of their favorite mini sliders before heading back to headquarters.

"Most cops get a bum rap for eating donuts but give me a good double White Castle with jalapeños any day and I'm a happy man," Tommy said sucking down one double slider in two quick bites.

Maggie couldn't ignore his ringing phone. "Aren't you going to answer that?"

He looked at his last bite of burger, smiled with reverence and popped it into his mouth, rubbing his greasy fingers on his napkin before swiping right on his phone.

"Yeah, Chief, we're done here, see you in a bit." He explained to Maggie that the FBI would be briefing the team on tonight's trap in about forty minutes, so their lunch break was over.

Chapter Fifty-Three

There was a frenetic energy when they entered the building. The anticipation of catching the Clergy Killer was palpable. It flooded the war room with nerves, anxiety, confidence, a stew of ingredients which had the target in their crosshairs. The strategy, the details, the exact timing and sequence must be plotted to perfection. Everyone needed to be on top of their game tonight and Special Agent in Charge Halsey was pacing the front of the room like a coach before the Final Four.

"Can we get settled, please?" He asked everyone to take a seat. He was playing to a packed house of detectives, his agents, Chief Bradshaw, a handful of select patrol officers, even the Commissioner and his press flunky showed up for the briefing.

"We only have a few hours to plot a trap for the Clergy Killer. If we don't get this right tonight, we risk him going underground, possibly for years.

"Everyone needs to be clear on every detail of the entire plan, even if your role is outside the church or back here at headquarters," Halsey continued.

Chief Bradshaw took the floor, explaining that Father Wampole of Saint Anthony's would be hearing confession tonight. "He is extremely nervous, as you can imagine, but he understands that this may be the only way to catch this guy."

Maggie and Tommy shared a glance, a knowing look between partners who could read each other's minds. Neither of them was convinced the Clergy Killer was a man. Something in their gut said it was a woman with some big-time daddy issues.

Father Wampole would be hidden in the confessional booth tonight. He would not look his would-be assassin in the eye, no face-to-face forgiveness. The open forum of modern-day confession didn't fit neatly into the trap and at some point, a detective could easily slide into Wampole's seat inside the confessional booth. If the killer was watching, they'd see the priest walk in but would never expect him to walk out...not in the middle of hearing confession.

Earlier in the day, Bradshaw had ironed out details with Cardinal Donohue so as not to have anyone other than a priest violating the sanctity and privilege of the sacrament. Once a detective took over inside, he would quickly assess and advise any penitent that he could not hear their sins tonight and they needed to leave. For most, they'd leave reluctantly, holding their secrets in their darkened souls for another shot at forgiveness tomorrow. For the killer, well, that just might be the spark to light his fury...and that's what they anticipated.

Bradshaw informed Tommy that he'd be the one to enter the confessional since the Clergy Killer was their case and Maggie, as a woman, couldn't be expected to hear confession.

"Holy, rock 'n' rolly, do I get to wear the collar to look the part?"

"No, but you get to wear a bullet-proof vest," Bradshaw answered quickly to diffuse any simmering annoyance on the part of the feds and the brass at the side of the room. But most of them were cops...once. They had to remember what it was like. They had to recall that wit and humor often got you to walk through that door when you didn't know what was waiting on the other side. Life or death?

"Remember, this unsub has been amped since the get-go," Special Agent Quinn said, outlining the suspect's behavior for the team. "His behavior resurrected another unsub, one who had been silent for more than fifteen years.

"That alone empowered the new unsub into an almost instant spree. He's killed four priests in four weeks and is feeling very much like he's in charge and this is his show.

"Anyone who threatens that power, anyone, not just the priest, may be in danger tonight."

Departmental regulations required anyone working the sting to wear a bullet-proof vest. Yet a wild shot, a bullet that ricochets, could easily enter wherever the protective Kevlar shield was missing. A lethal shot under the arm, in the head, in the femoral artery and it could be lights out. Despite the humor and in-house laughs, everyone in the room knew that was always a real serious threat.

"Maggie, you'll sit in the pew in the back corner, prayer veil, head down, while Lopez and Summers stand across the street, hanging out at the neighbor's house on Richardson Avenue. We've already advised the owners, so they won't be home," Bradshaw outlined the details and then reviewed them twice more.

Special Agent Sutton acknowledged the local detectives' suspicion that this unsub was a woman because of a failed love map with her own father but she wasn't convinced.

"Nothing in the kill pattern points to a woman. The unsub kills with military precision and knows enough to leave no trace behind.

"It's not that female serial killers are intentionally careless, but their motivation is much more passionate which often leads to a sloppy crime scene," Sutton continued.

"But when there's uncertainty, everyone's a suspect," she acknowledged. "Just look for anyone sketchy entering the church for confession tonight."

This is the Bronx. Sinners are sketchy.

Chapter Fifty-Four

Confession started at six and the crew arrived about thirty minutes early to stake out staging as much as to calm the nerves of the jittery Father Wampole.

"This is so unnerving," he admitted to Special Agent Sutton. "To think that someone wants to kill me not because of anything I've done but because of the collar I wear.

"What has this world come to?" He wondered aloud. Sutton didn't have an answer. She put herself to sleep every night with that same question on her mind. She woke every morning knowing all she could do was protect and serve.

Maggie took her place in the far corner of the last pew. The padding on the kneeler was so thin that she expected she'd be praying in a seated position if the stakeout lasted more than five minutes. She didn't think God meant for you to suffer when you came to his house to talk. She knows that was the church pablum they fed her at school for fourteen years but she didn't believe in her heart that it was God's plan. If God is a loving and forgiving God, then crippling the knees of his sorrowful children on wooden planks couldn't be part of his grand master plan for redemption. But these were questions for another night. This night the only plan was to take down the person killing God's earthbound messengers, even if they sometimes got his message wrong.

Come six o'clock, Father Wampole brushed aside the draped portal which gave him entry to the confessional. Tommy had already taken his place inside the booth, so the priest's entry was just for show. He snuck out almost immediately. The heavy velvet green curtain drape would do little to shield anyone who entered tonight. Even the Almighty couldn't keep death from his own door.

The black lace prayer veil covered all of Maggie's head and shoulders. They sent a clerk at headquarters up to the avenue to look for a shop selling old-fashioned *mantillas*. She was glad it was lace and not fabric since there was no air-conditioning inside the church and the lace allowed her to breathe with her head fully covered.

Maggie held a rosary in her hand, praying everyone stayed safe, realizing she had not held the blessed prayer beads since her Nonna's funeral two years ago. She heard her grandmother's voice in the silence, telling her to stay vigilant tonight. Nonna never understood why her only granddaughter had to become a cop, but she never asked the question more than once. It was Maggie's decision after all.

Maggie inhaled the stillness of the vast space, surrounded by emptiness and fake candles. *When did the church go fake?* She thought. When did they start using battery powered candles instead of flames to ignite inspiration? They said it was a safety issue but how many churches ever burned to the ground because of burning candles? Candlelight, especially fake, wasn't meant for death it was meant to inspire a hopeful life.

Fractured

Maggie wondered if God, the angels and saints even considered real prayers fed by fake candles. What a world indeed!

She texted Lopez who told her the street was just as dead outside as the church inside. Maybe the sinners of Saint Anthony's took the muggy night off.

"Pay no attention to the man behind the curtain," Tommy bellowed into the wired microphone on his lapel, simultaneously bored and on edge. He played with his team more to see if anyone was listening since no one was confessing a thing tonight, much less murder.

By eight o'clock, there wasn't a soul in the church except Maggie, Tommy and Father Wampole who exited the sacristy, his hiding place at the back, looking ashen and exhausted.

"Are you okay, Father?" Tommy asked as Wampole's facial expression was a banner of despair. The furrow across his forehead a sign of the weight on his soul. He was certain that even God's chosen disciples had their faith tested occasionally. Tommy himself felt the threat as he sat in the Father's place waiting for death to arrive, but it never did.

The team inside the FBI surveillance van included Assistant Chief Bradshaw who together with Special Agent Halsey decided to call off the sting at 8:30p. It was plenty enough time after confession ended for anyone to catch Father Wampole cleaning up and closing shop for the night. But the killer never came.

Bradshaw sent Summers and Lopez home and asked Tommy and Maggie to escort Father Wampole back to the rectory around the corner. They assured him there would be a patrol car outside all night. Things should be different in the morning but praying through the night might be the only way to wash away this fret-filled day.

Lisa Fantino

What do you see when you turn out the lights and you're all alone? Whose voice do you hear? He prayed through the silent night for salvation.

Chapter Fifty-Five

They both fought off exhaustion as they walked toward their cars. Sleep had been as elusive as a winning lottery ticket this past month. There comes a time, beyond the point of physical collapse, when adrenaline and bad coffee give you just enough of a boost to make it back home where the nap-wake cycle starts all over again until these killers are caught.

There wasn't an all-night diner waiting for them anywhere in Wakefield. A lot of greasy spoons. A lot of taquerias. But they just wanted a diner serving all-American staples, like burgers, grilled cheese and plenty of coffee. So, Maggie and Tommy followed each other up the Bronx River Parkway to the Sprain Parkway where they made their way down Jackson Avenue to the big Greek diner at the corner of Central Avenue. It was a circuitous route for a nutritional boost but when you're hungry and tired you don't always make the best decisions. Even meal choices weren't always the best.

"I'll have a Patty Melt and chocolate malted, not a shake, but a malted and a glass of water with a straw, please." Maggie spit it out without stopping to look at the menu. She still had the metabolism to eat like a teenager and not worry about losing her size six shape.

"Make that a double but I'll take a bottomless cup of your blackest coffee instead of a shake," Tommy said, "Oh, excuse me, maaalted." His imitation of Mags' order was sing-songy just to nudge her perfection. The pencil-thin waitress, with badly chipped red nail polish and wisps of hair coming from her ponytail pulled loosely into a scrungie, tilted her head toward Maggie and rolled her eyes. It was girl code for "this guy's got a clear head." It was okay. You only mock the ones you love, or so they say.

Even when they were off-duty they couldn't stop talking about the case. It consumed them from when they woke from their restless sleep to when their head dropped like a rock of exhaustion onto their pillows, and all the moments in between. It made it hard to interact with most other people. Even Tommy's wife knew better than to hand him a Honey-Do list when he was on a big case and this was as big as they come.

Something was off tonight. The trap was set perfectly but the timing or something else was off for the Clergy Killer who never showed.

"Serial Killers 101, kiddo," Tommy offered a teaching moment to his young partner. "They all have a pattern even when they think they don't."

"What?" She didn't know where he was going as she savored every bite of her greasy sandwich. She didn't know because she wasn't paying attention to him, not really. She just wanted to decompress. Then her inner switch flipped, as she washed down a bite with the chocolatey malted goodness in her glass.

"Oh my God, you're right," she stopped mid gulp and the moist glass nearly slipped from her fingers as it came to rest on the laminate table. "Why didn't you say something before they put this in motion."

"To be honest, it didn't really come to me until I was playing with myself in the confessional," Tommy said.

"Ewww, really, Tommy, the confessional?"

"Yes, in the logical progression of the killer's pattern, this next priest is likely to be killed in a confessional but it wasn't going to happen so quickly," Tommy suggested. "The priest killings so far have been confessional, basement, confessional, basement, which would make this one likely another hit inside the confessional but the timing is off. Something's not right," he said.

"Yeah, there was always a few days between when Binky's victim was found and when the next priest was killed," Maggie agreed.

Since Tiffany Paris was only found this morning, it was unlikely the next tag team kill would take place the same day. It didn't matter that she was already dead for a few days. If the priest unsub only hears about the crime in the news, when the public does, it takes him a few days to plot. He's not impetuous and certainly not sloppy. The only ones who seemed to be in a hurry this time were the people chasing the unsub's tail.

"Let's at least try to get a good night's sleep and make this discussion a priority in the morning," Tommy said.

They told each other to drive safely on the way home. There's even danger on the side roads if you fall asleep at the wheel.

Tommy let her take the lead heading north on Central Avenue. He had her back, or in this case, her rear fender as he watched her drive home. They were each falling into a special rhythm that takes some partners years to develop while others break up long before their relationship gels. But for Tommy and Maggie the bond had solidified quickly under the darkest of scenarios.

He was enjoying the mentoring role. It had been awhile since his partner was nearly half his age but so well-regarded for her instincts on the streets. She came to the division wanting to prove something but he was glad to see she was finally starting to give up her ghosts and the ones that haunted her revered father as well. To be a good detective, you had to be aware and live fully in the moment, even if the past played a role in the present. She was getting there.

Chapter Fifty-Six

June 30th

Her sheets were soaked with the nightmares of her sleep. She blamed the weather, not realizing her sleep was anything but restful while her waking hours were anything but productive. She thought this was normal. Everyone puts up with family, no matter what. Don't they?

Her timeworn nightgown stuck to her like a shroud as she rose out of her wet cocoon and made her way into the bathroom. She looked in the mirror but didn't recognize herself. Who had she become? What had he made her? Why had she allowed it to happen? Whenever it happened, however it occurred, she could only blame herself and only she could take care of it, once and for all.

She was too frugal to run the air conditioner unless the weather guy on TV declared it an official heat wave. Donovan was too disgusted to keep turning it on only to have her turn it off. The push and pull struggle between them had become unbearable…and extremely exhausting.

Donovan functioned mostly at night to keep his distance from her. He had free rein while she tried to sleep but he knew she struggled to find peace. His hardened shell made him invincible, impervious to the reality that wore her down.

Donovan could hear her showering, getting ready to start her day of torment against him. It was getting harder to live apart under the same roof. He would venture into the kitchen only when he was certain that she was hiding. But he had to eat, had to live, had to function. So, she would have to go. He was never more certain of anything.

She rummaged through her closet trying to find something light to wear. Summer seemed to arrive too quickly, although it came at the same time every year. This year, though, she had yet to switch her closet around making the seasonal clothes more accessible. She stretched for the top rod on the right, in the back, where her summer tops hung, color-coded and neatly pressed, just where she had put them last fall. It was only then that she noticed the loose ceiling tile on the left, slightly askew and out of its metal track. *Odd*, she thought, but she was too lethargic to even think about getting a step ladder from downstairs to fix it.

She pulled her hair up in a tight knot sweeping it off her face to stay cool. She barely had enough hair to gather it into a scrungie. It was mainly a messy bob, certainly not enough for a stylish ponytail. She didn't wear makeup or much jewelry, only her mother's ring, a small gold band with a sapphire, her birthstone, which she secured each night in the mirrored trinket box on her dresser. It was all she had left of a childhood sadly delinquent of much happiness or loving maternal memories.

Time passes, bad memories fade while the good ones remain, if you're lucky. If you're not, and good times were never had, you're in for a lifetime of misery and sadness. And for some, that can lead down a deadly path.

She reached for the heart-shaped box but as she lifted the lid to grab the memento, she froze. Ice ran through her veins.

226

Fractured

Oh yes, her mother's ring was there, tucked away, just where it should be, right next to a diamond pendant she had never seen before.

The usual litany of questions ran through her mind. Where did it come from? Who's been in my room? Who put it there? The only answer which rang true was Donovan.

She paced across her room, back and forth, back and forth, in a fury, plotting her attack. She had pulled and twisted at the loose wisps of bushy grey hair so much that her top knot came loose. She looked like an escapee from an asylum, twisting, fidgeting, mumbling incoherently and pacing, back and forth, back and forth. The threadbare area rug cried for mercy under her heft.

How dare he enter my space? Gotta get rid of him? Gotta get rid of him? He has to get out? He must get out.

Donovan knew when to stay quiet and when to let her know who's boss. Her frenetic, muddled rambling was the white noise inside his troubled mind. He had to silence it. *Dumb, stupid, whiny woman.* She droned on until he could take it no longer.

"Shut up, just shut up," he screamed loud enough to wake their mother in her grave, pulling at his own hair to stop the pain inside his head.

She was stunned silent, if only for a second.

"What's wrong with you?" He asked in the passive-aggressive exchange that had become the clumsy tango between them. One misstep and it was over. "You're a broken record. You've done nothing but bitch and stir up trouble since you retired. What's wrong with you?" He asked again not getting a response as quickly as expected.

"You're what's wrong with me," she sneered back. "You've always been what's wrong with me." She was on fire, pointing a finger at the image before her.

"You're always at the sidelines, watching, listening from behind closed doors. All these years I saw you…when you were watching…her…and them. You didn't think I knew but I saw everything…even *your* snickering like a silly little school boy.

"Mom told us to keep quiet inside the closet but you couldn't stand it. You couldn't listen to all the screaming, all the moaning. All you had to do was cover your ears." She was on a roll. She had never snapped back at him, not like this, not with the bitter venom spitting from her lips.

They lived the same life, traveled the same path but arrived at this moment quite differently. A shared recall manifesting in ways they didn't understand and in a verbal war they each struggled to control and ultimately win. The same moment, the same emotional abuse, viewed from the same black hole in the wall now exploding in a raging firestorm.

"Oh, you've learned nothing from me, nothing," he admonished her. "Guess I got all the smarts while hiding in the closet," he snickered, inciting her even more. She lashed out at him but he ducked from view to avoid her attack.

"You? What a joke? You've never held a job. Never had a friend. Never paid a bill.

"The only thing you're good at is knocking me." Her resentment was no longer blocked by any internal filter.

"Just look at you," she said standing in front of the mirror. "Do you see what I see?"

"Yeah, an old hag who's never been laid," Donovan continued his verbal castigation with mocking gestures, swaying back and forth, shoulders back, like he was cock of the walk.

Fractured

"I could kill you right now." She couldn't believe she said it, let the words fall from her lips so easily.

"Yeah, right, like that would ever happen," Donovan scoffed at her in the mirror.

She lashed out at him with a hiss, never turning her head but he was gone in an instant...and she was determined...to make him be gone forever.

Chapter Fifty-Seven

Friday of the long July Fourth holiday weekend meant nothing to the bone-tired team who dragged themselves into another morning meeting. This time Special Agent in Charge Halsey sprang for breakfast for everyone. The power struggle had yielded, if ever so slightly, to the greater good, to get the unsubs off the street before any more of God's children wound up dead.

"We jumped the gun here," Halsey admitted. It was a difficult thing to do for someone so rigid and so certain he was never wrong.

Chief Bradshaw let the room know that a protective detail had been with Father Wampole all night and would continue today. The cleric's busy schedule had him leaving the Bronx and heading into Manhattan tonight. He led a support group for the neighborhood's elderly homeless at Saint Malachy's for more than a decade, so the archdiocese let him continue even after his transfer to the Bronx.

"Guess we're spending a hot Friday night on the West Side, eh Chief?" Summers asked Bradshaw. Halsey and Bradshaw explained that the Midtown North precinct, as well as the Manhattan Detective Squad, were fully informed and

Fractured

onboard for assistance with tonight's stakeout. Halsey said the scenario would be almost the same as last night but hoped they had better results.

Bradshaw and Halsey explained that Wampole would be miked tonight and the entire team would be outside. That didn't sit well with Halsey or Chief Bradshaw. They liked having an agent or detective on the inside, but it wouldn't be, not tonight.

Father Wampole had explained that an outsider at this community meeting would stand out like an NBA player on a Tokyo subway, miles above the rest of the group. He couldn't have it. He wouldn't have it. He'd risk it all tonight for the people who needed him most.

He was the only logical choice as the next victim. The next priest to die had to come from Saint Anthony's and Father Wampole was the only resident priest left in the parish.

Another church lady wouldn't meet her maker until the Clergy Killer took revenge against those meant to protect and serve their flock. But that didn't mean Summers and Lopez would have the night off. They'd be on the street, ready to jump.

None of them had a day off in a month but murder never takes a holiday, not in the city that never sleeps and there'd be little sleep tonight.

Chapter Fifty-Eight

S he ventured into the light with more confidence this morning than she ever had since the day they were born. That dust-up between them pushed her over the edge into what she thought was a place of reason for justifiable homicide, a sin even God could forgive.

The mile-and-a-half-long journey down McLean Avenue from Yonkers into the Bronx and over the East 238th Street Bridge gave her time to think. The warm rays of the morning sun calmed her frayed nerves. She took her time, walking casually along the route she knew quite well. Not even the rush of morning traffic assaulted her senses. Her laser focus and sole purpose could not be violated by the mundane routine around her. Her motivation to end his life was the only thing that moved her forward, step by step, during the long walk.

She expected to scout out the parish schedule for confession but was surprised when she finally came upon Saint Anthony's Church that sinners could not fess up on Friday nights. *Now what?* Her focus was slightly fractured. This didn't work with her grand master plan, but she wouldn't be deterred.

An elderly woman, wearing nothing more than a thin housecoat, the edge of a slip hanging from its rear, approached her with a smile. Faded flowers with the scent of clean, sun-dried laundry perfumed the air around her as she pushed a shopping trolley toward the avenue. Her weekend food shopping was her only chore for the day. Life was so simple and easy for some, while others swirled in a pool of torment.

She asked the old woman when the church would be open and learned that no one was around on Fridays after morning mass. Father Wampole was the only priest in the rectory and tonight was his night to counsel the aging homeless at Saint Malachy's in Manhattan.

Manhattan? Her plans were frustrated at every turn. The thought of venturing into a foreign neighborhood, into a church she didn't know, placed her well out of her comfort zone. The tranquility she had enjoyed on her morning walk had been replaced by an uneasiness, a level of unpredictability that set the stage for unplanned encounters and sloppy mistakes. Decisions she hadn't anticipated. Something as simple as taking the train downtown flustered her.

She tried to regain her composure as she walked up to White Plains Road to catch the bus back home. The heat and humidity were rising with her level of discomfort. She wasn't still within herself and her fidgeting fingers displayed an anxious woman to the old man sitting next to her. He had no escape as she twirled the fingers of both hands like she was playing an imaginary piccolo. The cool bus was crowded with the heat of people seeking relief. The more she thought about her task ahead tonight, the faster the fidgeting became and the quicker the old gent moved to step off at the next stop.

Maybe, just maybe, I'll feel better when I cool off. She thought. She was oblivious to the hovering crowd in the congested aisle. She needed to regain mental direction if she was going to pull off the biggest hit of her life. And she needed to do it quickly. Time was not on her side.

Chapter Fifty-Nine

The incessant hum of the air-conditioner was the only sound she heard as she walked into the house. It had cooled the house considerably in her absence. She couldn't let Cuddles melt on a day like today. Even her frugality yielded to childish indulgences at times. She knew it was the right thing to do, the right thing for her, as his fluffy little body ran up to caress her ankles. She stood in the foyer, surveying all that she knew, all that was both right and wrong in her world.

There was a frigid stillness that filled the space. She couldn't see or hear Donovan but the threat of his presence haunted her like the reality of knowing we're all going to die. It's a commonality, a certainty for all of us. It's just a matter of when.

If he was hiding, she didn't care. She had given up caring a long time ago. The pain of unappreciated consideration, even without the hope of anything in return, was wearisome. After tonight, he'd be nothing more than an afterthought, a punctuation mark on their entire wretched lives together.

Fractured

Liberation waited on the horizon. She was just hours away from knowing the peace she sought for more than fifty years. He was just hours away from final damnation.

Her laser-driven purpose steered a different course for her tonight. No more penny-pinching. No more worrying about others knowing her route. No more fretting whether he was following. Tonight, she called a taxi to shuttle her to the Woodlawn train station for her last journey to a new existence.

An eerie countenance had washed over her like a restorative bath at an ancient spa. The midday fidgeting was replaced by a pleasant calm. A young man with a violin case didn't hesitate to sit next to her. She smiled not at him but for herself. She enjoyed the prospect of conducting her own symphony. He was unaware of the music only she could hear.

Chapter Sixty

People crowded into Times Square like busy ants, all moving somewhere but still trapped in the same spot. Men, women, kids, sinners, even killers and the angels among us filling the hustle and bustle of the Theater District all looking up, not looking ahead which is the only place for forward momentum. Look up, look back and you'll trip on where you've been.

The team of Bronx detectives and federal agents had tripped up big time last night, wasting a stakeout with no results. It happens. So, you move on and get over it. Yet, here they were now, in the center of the universe, or so New Yorkers would tell you, with millions of people unaware they were trying to take down a serial killer. They had one goal tonight. Take down one while protecting millions.

The swarm of innocents on a Friday night meant they had to park their stakeout early, mark their turf. Even undercover cops fight for parking on congested streets. The guys at Midtown North assisted them by staking out some prime spots opposite the church using police cones and two patrolmen to stand guard as of three o'clock. After all, truckers and well-heeled New York drivers could and would squeeze their car between cones like nobody's business, not thinking for a moment that the police cones blocking a space were meant for them.

The feds were the first to arrive in their *Sweet Treats Bakery* van presumably to make deliveries to area restaurants. They swapped out different magnetic business signs to slap onto the side of the vehicle as the need arose. But many observant people, at least those used to cops in big cities, could spot a police van a mile away. There's just something about a white van painted with the logo of a bakery that no one's ever heard of that just sticks out...no matter where you park it! Don't you think?

The van pulled up at four, the patrolmen carefully removing the orange cones to allow easy parking access. Did Special Agent in Charge Halsey or Assistant Chief Bradshaw really think this was incognito? A quick peek inside the open van door would reveal a hive of worker bees, electronics to rival a network newsroom and not a donut, pastry or sweet treat in sight.

Detectives Summers and Lopez were also supposed to be undercover, to blend in with their surroundings of miscreants and tourists. They were ordered to grab a seat at the window ledge inside the expensive coffee shop opposite the church. With radio earpieces designed to look like geeky earbuds, they were supposed to appear like two guys waiting to start their weekend, listening to the game, music or waiting for some chick's call. Yet they needed to watch and listen carefully, very carefully amid their noisy surroundings. They had to monitor the audio track from Father Wampole's microphone as well as take orders from central command inside the van.

Maggie and Tommy sat in their steamy squad car parked opposite the church and the adjacent garage where Father Wampole had parked his car. Just in case he was ambushed after leaving the church, the killer would have no place to hide. But sitting outside Broadway's Eugene O'Neill Theater was no way to disappear into the shadows, not with people picking up last minute tickets for tonight's show. In just a few short hours, the curtain would rise on a night most of them would never forget.

"In another three hours, this place will be swarming with hundreds of theatergoers," Maggie stating the obvious for Tommy. "It's a friggin' takedown nightmare."

"Ahh, most of them will think they've walked onto the set of "Law and Order." He was always ready to lighten the load and tonight's was extra heavy.

The waiting was never easy, the uncertainty, the discomfort of sitting on sticky vinyl car seats for hours on end unable to run the air conditioner for as long as they'd be parked. The evening wouldn't provide much relief from the heat under the prolonged day of an early summer night. The sun wouldn't set until at least nine o'clock and they were hoping to snare a killer by then. No, this was one important stakeout in broad daylight on a congested street in midtown.

Detectives Tommy Martin and Maggie Flynn hadn't been together long, but this case was anointing their new partnership quickly with the daily grind of long hours spent together. You run out of things to say when you spend that much time together under any circumstances, so the pair sat in silence staring into the void of congestion.

They had all tested and retested their mikes numerous times, confirming to stay attentive as directed by Bradshaw in the van, checking in with a firm "Roger that" or "10-4." Then it was back to mind-numbing browsing of the webbed abyss on their cell phones while they waited for whom they didn't know.

Fractured

The sudden rumble of thunder shook them all awake, made them realize a storm was coming, made them realize even God was unhinged tonight as they sat on the edge of Hell's Kitchen.

They had stocked up with a case of water and sandwiches before parking into place. They knew the night would be long and without a bathroom in sight they would need to carefully balance the need to stay hydrated with the impulse to relieve themselves. Not even the well-pressed feds were immune from the calls of Mother Nature.

"It's ironic," Maggie said as the clouds finally dropped buckets of rain, the noise on the hood and the roof of the car so deafening that she nearly had to shout to make herself heard over the din.

"What is?" Tommy slouched in his seat more to relax into the wait rather than to hide from a dangerous unsub. They were out in the open looking very much like the cops they were.

"We're teetering on the edge of Hell's Kitchen waiting to take down the anti-Christ.

"Don't you find that odd?" Maggie commented on the New York neighborhood that got its name as a place so tough to live in the late 19th Century that only the devil himself could be in charge. She multi-tasked her thought process more often than not. She could see the analytical, the factual and even the philosophical meaning behind almost anything if she pondered long enough. That's what made her a good detective. That's what made women different from men, at least just one of the things. Women and men just think differently.

"Yeah, okay," Tommy responded as most men would, dismissive of anything that wasn't black and white and sitting in front of them.

They could barely see now as the rain fell in blinding sheets. It was the kind of deluge that was anticipated when the barometer fell so low and lingered so long. The air squeezed the atmosphere under its weight until the heavens yielded. They hoped their target didn't slither into the community center while they were at such a blinding disadvantage.

Chapter Sixty-One

It was a brief thirty-minute walk from Grand Central. The heat wave had finally broken with a restorative thunderstorm during her train ride downtown. The tension in the air, that static electricity which lobs cloud to ground lightning like daggers from the heavens, was no longer a threat. In fact, she imagined a lovely sunset tonight as she walked westward on 42nd Street.

The smell of ozone after the rain masked the true scent of this gritty neighborhood on a hot summer evening. Even Times Square took on a lovely aura as the sun set over midtown, sparkling with the shine of the earlier storm. She stepped through puddles of light as neon billboards and taxi headlights reflected a fake life on her beaten path.

Her early arrival gave her time to scout out Saint Malachy's Community Center, where she'd find Father Wampole in another ninety minutes or so. She could see only the one door where the signage indicated the time for tonight's gathering. It looked unassuming, a lower level annex to the hundred-year-old church now showing its age. The indigent and trash decorated its steps with empty beer bottles now full of mystery moisture, a toxic soup of someone's relief from the night before. Her life, desperate and lonely, had prepared her for this very moment. She didn't need to muster confidence. Tonight, she was as strong as Joan of Arc and knew what she must do. She was on a relief mission of her own, but she wasn't expecting sainthood.

Greasy spoons had yielded to boutique coffee shops on nearly every corner in the Broadway area. She grabbed a stool in the window at one of them with a perfect view of the community center across the street. She bought herself a coffee and did what all New Yorkers do, people-watch, imagining what brought them to that exact spot at that moment in time.

The very set-up of the ledge seating was meant to isolate those who just wanted a spot to sip a tea or coffee and chill. Sometimes you find yourself lost in the thick of city life crowded with mobile billboards, limousines and biked messengers, the homeless garbed in rags and the tourists clothed in tacky Big Apple T-shirts. You just need a space to regroup. Coffee shops had become the perfect place to fade into the crowd, unaware that an undercover cop...or two...may be one seat over.

She caught her reflection in the window and realized she fit right in with her surroundings. She looked like a hooded bag lady wearing ill-fitting, pull-on knit pants and dollar store sneakers. She wasn't homeless, but tonight she might as well be. Her only care was whether Donovan would survive till morning.

She was ready. She knew she was. She even brought the cat to the house next door and gave the neighbor's kid ten bucks to cat sit. Cuddles shouldn't suffer for her sins the way she had for their mother's. Animals take care of their own. Humans could take a lesson from them.

Fractured

She was very much alone, isolated in her conviction. Her only companion tonight was Pearl, two women with one purpose.

Chapter Sixty-Two

Father Wampole was leading a group tonight outside the privacy of a confessional or the anonymity of a twelve-step program. No privilege to cross. Nothing to violate except the sanctity of life. His community support meeting was more a social gathering, a place to connect for the disenfranchised elderly, a place to connect with other people who knew them and cared about them, even if only for one night a week.

He agreed to be miked only with the understanding that the police monitor his audio track from outside the building. The chief acquiesced. He had no choice. It was the priest's way or no way.

True, a life could be snuffed out in the instant it would take the cops to jump out of a squad car and into the building, but Wampole was willing to risk that to give his group the comfort it needed. He didn't want his usual suspects to be made ill-at-ease by outsiders who were better dressed. Cardinal Donohue stuck by the priest's decision from the cushioned, secured comfort of his majestic stone fortress, waiting for an end to the latest scandal to blight the city's Catholic institution.

Fractured

The smell of urine assaulted her nostrils, she felt the bile rise up in her gullet as she entered the building. She could barely contain the urge to gag. *God, these people are sick*, she thought to herself, resenting that she had to endure their mental illness, not realizing her own. There had to be a way to clean up the city's homeless. City Hall was clearly undoing all that had been cleaned off the streets twenty-five years ago. But after tonight, it would no longer be her problem or her concern.

She spied a dark corner in the hall where she could sit and rock and mumble. Everyone, even the crazies, would leave a mumbling rocker alone. Everyone's got a bit of crazy inside them. No one needs an extra helping. And with this being called The Actor's Chapel, they'd think she was rehearsing a role.

But this was no dress rehearsal. She might appear loopy and insane but she had never been more lucid or well-prepared in her life.

Chapter Sixty-Three

Maggie and Tommy listened to Father Wampole's audio track in their car while the FBI and Assistant Chief Bradshaw listened in the van and Summers and Lopez were ready to assist from the comfort of the coffee bar. They could all hear quite well as those inside the community center connected as if for the first time after a long absence.

"Did you hear, Lucy got attacked last night at the shelter?"

"Poor girl. I won't go there."

"Me neither. I like my place just fine."

"Where ya livin' now?"

"Oh, you know, down on Riverside."

They were greetings without a connection. Conversations without substance. Chats without revelations. That was life on the streets. *New York, just like I pictured it!*

They monitored Father Wampole's microphone as well as several others placed in and around the room. By the voices they heard, they guestimated about twelve to fifteen people in attendance of various ages. Both sexes seemed to be well-represented. They realized it was only an educated guess because there were always some people in a crowd, especially a gathering of debilitated and infirmed members of society, who didn't feel secure enough to speak out.

Why is it the poor, the mentally ill, the down-on-their-luck never feel the need to broadcast their situation to the world while rich celebrities believe it's their obligation to share their most intimate secrets? Why is it those who need help the most, on so many levels, contain their inner turmoil, carrying their burden in a quiet dignity, while those with the world at their fingertips use their troubles to secure another fifteen minutes in the spotlight? Just who faces the bigger problem?

"There's a lot you can learn from a voice, just a voice," Maggie said. She understood the complexities of the human psyche often well beyond her years. She was always thinking beyond what was apparent in most situations.

"You can tell if someone's scared or under stress. And if they're happy, there's a lilt in their voice," she said.

"As opposed to the lint on their clothing," Tommy chimed in.

"What?" He shrugged in response. He responded to her skeptical, questioning eyes with a smirk. "I'm a visual person. Men have to see to understand."

"Oh, yeah, there's a lot men need to understand and they still don't get it...most of the time," Maggie speaking as the voice of most women.

"My dear partner, you'll remain a spinster for your whole life with that attitude!

"You know, with all of your questioning and probing and observing, you would have made a great reporter, like your friend Mickey Malone," Tommy suggested.

"Or a great detective," she deadpanned making a finger check-mark in the air over the dashboard as if they were keeping score on the volley of *bon mots*.

"That too." He couldn't agree more.

Tommy wondered what actually went on in a support group that wasn't really a support group. Fortunately, he had never gone to such a gathering. He'd never been to therapy. Sure, he had discharged his weapon many times in the line of duty but most of his spot-on target work had been at the shooting range and he was blessed that he had never taken a life, so the need to purge emotions wasn't a pressing concern.

"What do you think they do in there?" He wondered.

"Hold hands and sing Kumbaya," Summers chimed in. They each forgot they could hear one another on their earpieces along with the group sharing trivialities inside.

"Let's pay attention, folks," Halsey reminded them. "Our unsub could be in there already."

Paying attention yielded little information they could use quickly sitting outside. They listened as those in the support group meeting exchanged more stories about the soup kitchen, nightmares about the shelter and complaints about where to sleep tonight since their cardboard box shacks had probably been ruined by the earlier downpour.

The rich worry about how many houses they own. Hell, in fact, if they're rich enough they pay people to worry for them. The middle class worries about keeping a roof over their heads. And these poor souls worry about not having a roof at all. Life, like anything else, is all about perspective.

After an hour of engaging with one another, Father Wampole thanked everyone for coming and invited them back next week. Shuffling feet, chairs sliding, doors opening and closing, the mumble of too many people talking at once and the occasional goodbye shouted above the crowd noise were all a part of the soundtrack that ended their story tonight.

"You never know when the last goodbye will come," Maggie said, "...with anyone."

Chapter Sixty-Four

Pop, pop, pop. The shots shattered Maggie's thoughts of goodbye. She and Tommy were out of their squad car faster than a final farewell could cross their lips.

Summers and Lopez hightailed it out the coffee shop. All had guns drawn, at the ready and pointed down, as they charged toward the church building, darting between anxious passersby who jumped out of the way, some grabbing shelter at the sight of four armed lunatics. The crowd had no idea they were in the middle of a real-life police drama. A guy on the corner searched for TV cameras in hopes of grabbing his quick fifteen minutes of fame.

Maggie and Tommy breached the unlocked door, looking left and right, high and low, as they crossed the five-foot darkened hall toward the main meeting room. Summers and Lopez covered them shortly behind, chasing the last few stragglers from the hall and out into the night where patrol officers were ordered to stop anyone exiting the building for questioning.

Tommy pushed the swinging door inward until it clicked in an open position. No bullets flew in his direction as he entered. Maggie followed, quick on his heels. Their hearts were pumping faster than a tornado ready to mow down anything in its path. The life and death decisions they make happen in less than a nanosecond. There was no time to hesitate, no time to think, you just do it. It's instinctual after so much time on the job. You're sure of your focus before you make your first move, before you breach the door. To slip, to hesitate, to back down even for an instant may mean someone dies today.

Their radios were live. Everything they did or said was amplified in the van for Halsey and Bradshaw, who were audio witnesses as the scene played out.

"Wampole down, I repeat Wampole is down," Tommy said as he neared the priest lying on his side on the floor, his back toward the exit, his face turned away as he and Maggie approached cautiously.

They entered through the only door in the small basement room. So, unless the killer was one of the stragglers now being held streetside by patrolmen, where was he?

Tommy heard Father Wampole moan and groan as he neared the downed cleric on the black and white vinyl floor. His blood wasn't pooling which was a good sign. Maybe the wound wasn't serious.

"What the hell?" Tommy screamed out as another body revealed itself once he could see beyond the bulk of Wampole's body in the dimmed lights of the basement.

"We need a boss and a bus, a boss and a bus, ASAP," Maggie yelled into her radio.

Summers and Lopez entered the space as back-up after ascertaining there was no one lingering in the halls or the restrooms. Anyone who mattered now was inside this space which just minutes ago was filled with the spontaneity of life and which now echoed with the finality of death.

Maggie's gun was pointed down at the ready position as she viewed the other body on the floor and searched her surroundings for the possible shooter. Her left hand supported her right to steady herself and her weapon. She was certain she would take and ultimately get the shot to take down this suspect. She could see blood and brain matter oozing from what was left of the black-hooded body. She was certain death was at her feet. No one could lose that much brain matter and still be alive.

Tommy was engaging with Father Wampole who didn't appear too seriously hurt and was getting all the assurances he needed from the seasoned detective crouching next to him. Tommy had glanced up at Maggie, watching out for his partner, who assured him with a hand gesture and nod toward the pool of ooze at her feet that the other downed person was a goner. But whether it was another victim or the unsub, she couldn't be sure.

Summers and Lopez had circled Maggie, protecting her as they would any other guy on the job but understanding that she might need a touch more extra support this time around because it was her first big homicide...and it was a doozy. Their guns were also at the ready just in case this unsub gave up something more than a throaty death rattle in his last step toward a painful eternity.

Maggie stepped carefully around the pool of ooze which was now spreading away and toward the front of the bloody mass before her. Her weapon was still in her shooting hand. She wouldn't holster it until she was sure the suspect was dead and no longer a threat to her or anyone else on the team. It had to be the shooter. No one else had time to flee in the melee as

251

the cops sequestered anyone who tried to leave. She'd have to brush the hoodie aside at least to get a pulse reading at the base of the neck near his carotid artery.

She turned to look up at Detective Lopez as he called her name.

"Mags, here," he held out a glove which he'd taken from his pocket and tossed it to her. "We gotcha," he assured her, indicating she could put her gun away and glove up before reaching into bloody hell. Summers and Lopez hovered directly over her and the body. This guy wasn't getting away, not tonight, not ever.

With the middle and index fingers of her right hand, now gloved, she reached down to slide the hoodie back. So much blood, it was everywhere.

"This guy must've eaten his own gun," Maggie said in astonishment. Most of his face, at least the side closest to Maggie, was gone.

"OK, Mags, get out of there," Summers said, as he offered a hand up off the floor. "Let forensics take over."

"What's going on in there? Talk to me," a frustrated Halsey blurted orders into their earpieces. But before anyone could answer, Special Agents Quinn and Sutton were already inside the building.

Wampole was sitting up, drawing everyone's attention.

"I think she missed me on purpose," he offered his assessment.

"She?" Quinn questioned him in disbelief.

"Yes, the shooter was a woman. She came out of nowhere," he continued revealing details but still very much in shock. He explained that she must have been hiding in the hall during the session and only made her way in when she was sure everyone was out of the room.

"'Father,' she called out to draw my attention," Wampole explained that he first saw her when he turned to answer. "She stood about four feet away and fired right at my shoulder before placing the gun in her own mouth and pulling the trigger." There was no time to stop her but why would he want to? Even the holy are tested...sometimes more than they ever expected.

Chapter Sixty-Five

Outside had become as much of a nightmare as downstairs in the church basement. It's not easy shutting down a street in Manhattan on a moment's notice, much less a busy side street in the Theater District on a Friday night in the summer. Pandemonium was a real possibility. People scurried away when they saw the agents, guns blazing, running from the van. Others ran toward the craziness with phone cameras recording trying to cash in on someone else's misery. That had sadly become the norm in the 21st Century.

People had become so desensitized to a fading common morality and sense of respect for each other and for law enforcement. How do you hear shots fired and not worry about yourself and those around you? How is it that your first thought in a crisis is to see how you can make money selling video footage to any media vulture willing to buy their news? What happened to responsible journalism, asking questions and vetting sources before rushing to judgment. Crazy greed is the new norm.

Fractured

This was an impossible situation to contain. Police cordoned off the area, which itself drew more people to that very spot, more journalists asking more questions but detectives and the feds had very few answers.

Assistant Chief Bradshaw, from command ops inside the van, called anyone and everyone from Midtown North to CSU and the Medical Examiner. It would be all hands on deck to deal with the dead unsub and corral the onlookers searching for who-knows-what.

This was a logistics nightmare. Summers and Lopez were already topside, assisting officers taking statements from the meeting attendees. The church had opened its doors to the upper chapel to provide a place for these people to be questioned, away from onlookers, cameras and the discomfort of knowing someone just violated the one space they thought they'd be secure.

They couldn't order businesses to shutter their doors but some of those businesses took up vital space inside the parameters of central command. There was no time to tow the pedestrian vehicles out of their illegal spots as the forensic team and guys from the morgue all showed up with their own vans squeezing into the congested one-way street. At the very least, Bradshaw ordered all media trucks to be stopped at the corner of Broadway and 49th Street, east of the scene, and at the corner of Eighth Avenue and 49th Street just to the west. Even if intrepid reporters and their crews decided to hoof it down the street with cameras in tow, they'd still be kept at least half a block away from Saint Malachy's. Local patrol had already set up a perimeter with yellow crime scene tape and stood sentry in case anyone tried to sneak by. If theatergoers stepped out for a smoke at intermission or exited when the show ended, they'd be funneled down the block by a line of patrol officers.

This was big. No. This was huge. Speculation had already made its way to the city's two all-news stations which man their newsrooms with desk assistants monitoring the police scanner. Bradshaw heard it first on 1010 WINS.

"There may be a break in the Clergy Killer case," the news anchor announced to the world knowing nothing more than the desk assistant gleaned from the scanner. Responsible vetting at its finest. Let's get it on the air first. Who cares if it's accurate? "At this hour, police may have a suspect barricaded inside a church in Times Square," the anchor continued. Special Agent in Charge Halsey abruptly turned off the inaccurate babble before joining Bradshaw in the hub of activity outside the van.

"Barricaded? Dead is more like it," Bradshaw voiced his frustration. It was the first thing Halsey could agree on since this started. They also both knew without a doubt that this would be the lead that bleeds on the eleven o'clock news and that was less than three hours from now.

Chapter Sixty-Six

"Did you ever see her before?" Maggie asked Father Wampole as he sat in a chair, his flesh wound on his shoulder being dressed by paramedics before they transported him to the Mount Sinai West Hospital.

"No, not here, not anywhere," he said. "At first it was hard to tell she was a woman, but I heard it in her voice. It was soft, not gruff, just older...and quite calm, considering," his thoughts trailed off.

"Then she said something that didn't make sense but in the flash of that moment nothing made sense."

Maggie understood. Police were trained to operate at a heightened sense of awareness to take it all in at once when life was rapidly firing before them. But for the average Joe, the average priest, the pieces are all jumbled when life flashes before you. She probed him to explain, to close his eyes and focus on that moment when crazy just exploded in front of him.

"She apologized," he said. His facial expression contorted in skepticism.

"What were her exact words?" Maggie implored him for details. "Please close your eyes and focus. I know it's hard." She questioned Wampole while the details were still fresh in his head, at the forefront of his evening and not a week down the line. The further they moved away from tonight, the foggier his recollection would be. Would the experience be clouded with either the grey pall of a frightful memory or colored with the vibrancy of questionable journalistic accounts? Either way, his thoughts would be tainted by life.

"She apologized," he said again. "She said 'I'm sorry' as she pointed the gun at me." He explained further that he could hear her still mumbling as he fell to the floor with his head turned toward her. They were details he'd rather forget but that would forever be etched in his memory. All he wanted was to leave this place and not come back. He never signed up for this in the seminary.

"Did she say anything further?" Maggie sounded like a broken record but that was her job to prod and poke and probe and search for the answers to all the open-ended questions. There were more than most because this was more than most, not one homicide but dueling killers in a fight for notoriety. Or, was it much more than a superficial fight to the end?

"Just before she placed the gun in her mouth she said, 'this ends with me, tonight'." Wampole hoped this was the end of the investigation for now.

The thickness of the basement air now growing dank, bordering on putrid, as they remained in the midst of it. There was a dead body sitting in a pool of ooze in the heat of a basement room without an air conditioner. The crowd inside was also growing larger, sucking up whatever airspace was available. Federal agents, detectives, patrol officers, forensics and the M.E.'s staff had crowded in like maggots to death in a feeding frenzy.

Maggie took notes as the priest continued until her partner's voice rang out in shock.

Fractured

When she turned in his direction, ready to draw and shoot if necessary, he was hovering over the hooded corpse as the forensics crew collected evidence and captured photos of the scene.

"Maggie, get over here," he yelled to her. His voice emphatic, demanding, not inviting.

"You're not gonna believe this," he said, his eyes never leaving the bloody mass at his feet. His mouth agape. A vision he never expected.

Maggie could see the investigators had rolled the body onto its back but all she could see from her vantage point was a bloody pile in front of her about fifteen feet away. As she stepped closer, quickly, she realized all the implications.

"Oh my God," she gasped, her mouth also hung in disbelief. Could her eyes be deceiving her? After all, she hadn't slept properly in over a month.

"Emma?" She looked up at Tommy. The quizzical expression in her eyes reflected back at her through his. "Emma? Why Emma?" It was the one question they hadn't anticipated and the one question whose answer may lead them to solve a string of homicides decades in the making.

Here in the heart of Times Square, on a steamy summer night, they got their girl...but where was her adversary?

Chapter Sixty-Seven

The investigation, which had dragged on for six weeks or more, was now rapidly evolving. Where was the Binky Killer? How did he know Emma? Were they related? Had they worked together? Was it also someone inside the NYPD? Was he close at hand, maybe in the crowd outside? Was he watching or working the case? Did he even know she was dead? These were the questions that plagued the team of federal and local investigators who knew it would be a race to find him.

Assistant Chief Bradshaw needed his team to tackle the heavy-lifting while he met with the Chief, Commissioner, Mayor and spoke with Ray Peretti at Saint Pat's. Oh, there'd certainly be the obligatory media gang bang in less than two hours and he was going to keep a close lid on which details were released.

He directed Summers and Lopez to continue with the on-scene investigation at Saint Malachy's, questioning witnesses and Father Wampole after he was released from the hospital. He knew the feds were going to get to Emma's house, eventually, but he wanted his team there first. This was their case, his squad. They had spent countless hours on a treadmill to nowhere until this very moment. Why shouldn't they be the ones to tie it up in a bow?

But what about the Binky Killer? Speculation was front and center for Summers and Lopez. That was their case but until they got a handle on just what happened with Emma tonight, they couldn't run around the boroughs hoping that the Binky Killer would appear out of the darkness. No, they had to wait...wait until he was good and ready to show them his hand.

Chapter Sixty-Eight

Carefully, cautiously, they squirmed their way through the crowd outside, trying to get to their squad car before Halsey's team stopped them. Maggie and Tommy only answered to Bradshaw and it would be his knot to untangle once the FBI realized his detectives were already light years ahead, speeding up the West Side Highway to Yonkers. With sirens blazing, they could make it there in thirty minutes...if they were lucky with Friday night traffic.

Chief Bradshaw had already called the judge on duty for a search warrant which he'd send to Tommy and Maggie in the car by the time they made it to Westchester. He also called the Yonkers Police Department, giving them a heads up that his detectives would be taking the door at Emma's house within the hour, warrant in hand. He didn't need to remind his suburban counterparts that this was an evolving homicide case and nothing was to be leaked, radios were to be silent. After all, the Binky Killer was still out there. They weren't going to lose him a second time.

"So much for the profilers," Maggie snipped in the car, in the privacy of their own confessional, where partners tell each other everything.

Fractured

She was having an *atta girl* moment, even if she was patting her own back. Her gut, her Godfather, Tommy and their endless games of Clue over a month ago all pointed to the Clergy Killer being a woman with daddy issues.

"It takes a lot to shock the hell out of me," Tommy said, "but this is one for the books.

"She had some poker face, never gave it up, never looked nervous.

"She made us iced tea for Chrissake!" They both marveled at Emma's composure not only during their probing visit with her a few weeks ago but during her many visits to One PP. So many cops, not a one with any clue about the killer among them...and now they wondered if there was another one still on the loose.

Maggie was busy riding shotgun but took time to send Uncle Bobby a quick text, letting him know she was safe. She also texted Tommy's wife Helen knowing he wouldn't do it. He was on a case. He'd get home late and Helen would be pacing, furious that he couldn't find thirty seconds to let her know she could rest easy on that pillow they shared for twenty-five years. At least until the next time.

Maggie understood because she had been the little girl in a single-family home, always praying her Daddy would come home whenever he left for work. So Maggie had this covered. She texted both their families because that's what partners do. The story would be breaking on the eleven o'clock news and Bobby and Helen would be pacing until they heard from them. Worry came with the territory when you loved a cop but taking the worry away...when you could...was inherent in the job description, easing a troubled mind so you could get on with the task at hand.

And you just never know what goes on in someone's mind, no matter how they appear on the outside. It's what's swirling in their heart, in their soul, in the dusty crevices of their past that bubble to the surface leaving an unsuspecting public at their mercy.

They had the gun, finally. Maggie and Tommy didn't have to wait for the ballistics reports to know the bullets shot tonight would be a perfect match to those which claimed the lives of Fathers McNamara, Wojcick, Torres and Rodriguez. Tonight, Emma spared Wampole to write the final chapter in her own murder mystery.

Chapter Sixty-Nine

The porch was dark. The lights were out. Nobody was home as Tommy pulled right up in front of Emma's house. It was a tiny cottage-style home, nearly a hundred-years-old, that survived the development of the neighborhood around it. It survived because it had a solid foundation, or did it?

Neighbors moved in and out of semi-detached homes which lined the block, revealing no personality of their architect and no clues of the secrets each of us locked away behind closed doors. What secrets did Emma keep? What lessons would detectives learn tonight about the killer living in their midst?

"This street won't be quiet for long," Maggie observed as they approached the front steps. The two Yonkers police officers, who had been waiting on the porch in the darkness, introduced themselves to Maggie and Tommy. The one holding the Halligan tool stepped up to force entry through the door. Maggie had called for help on the ride up when they realized the door-busting tool wasn't in their trunk.

It was surreal. A prim and proper home decorated in lace and wicker was a hellish killer's lair. The incongruity of prim and proper with the bloody and deadly trail Emma left behind wasn't lost on the four crimefighters taking it all in for the first time.

They were barely inside the living room, no more than five minutes, when there was a knock on the front screen door, the lock plate now torn from the inner door jamb by the forced entry. Maggie looked down to see a tiny thing, no more than seven or eight-years-old holding Emma's cat lovingly in her arms.

"Well, who do we have here?" Maggie asked the towheaded child who was shadowed on the steps by a woman, most probably her mother. After all, any responsible mom wouldn't let a child so young go out after dark and it was just after nine o'clock.

Maggie bent down to speak directly with the little girl on her level so as not to intimidate the child.

"I'm Hailey," the tiny, blond curly-top said with a smile. "Ms. Emma asked me to babysit for Cuddles, so I was just bringing him home.

"We saw the lights on," she said.

"We live next door," the mom chimed in from the bottom step.

Maggie explained that Emma wasn't home and asked Hailey if she'd like to continue watching the cat if that was okay with her mom. All agreed and Hailey was directed to bring the cat back to her own home and her dad while Maggie spoke with her mother, Jill Stonington.

"Has something happened to Emma?" Jill asked as she sat on the edge of the only porch chair, the lights still out so as not to draw attention. Jill, however, could see this was serious. The three men inside must be cops, she thought to herself, they all had guns strapped to their shoulders or around their waists, even this woman. She saw the badge glisten in the darkness as Maggie introduced herself.

Fractured

"I'm Detective Margaret Flynn, NYPD, but you can call me Maggie," she said. "Yes, Miss Kelly has died."

"Oh my God," Jill said falling back into the chair. "Where, when…what happened?"

Maggie explained that she couldn't say more but that it would really help if Jill wouldn't mind answering a few questions.

The brief conversation revealed what they already knew. Emma lived alone and didn't have any family. A quiet lady who kept to herself and who cherished her cat.

"It was odd, though, just today," Jill explained that hindsight now gave clarity to her earlier impression. "It was strange.

"She never asked Hailey to cat sit before. She paid her and everything…paid her well.

"It was almost as if she didn't plan to come back."

"Just one other thing before I let you get back to Hailey," Maggie stopped the eager-to-leave neighbor rising from the chair. "Did she have many, or any, visitors?"

"No, not really, although in the past few weeks I'd often hear her screaming with a man, fighting," Jill said. "I'd look out the window for a while when it happened because they were loud, really loud, but it never lasted long, and I never saw him coming or going."

Maggie thanked her, gave Jill her card and said they'd be in touch if they had any further questions. What she really wanted to do was give the nice woman a heads up on the media circus about to descend on their neighborhood. But that wasn't her job, she had enough to do tonight.

CSU had arrived shortly after them. Bradshaw had all his ducks in a row and made sure they were all doing their jobs.

267

Even back at headquarters, Bradshaw had desk clerks running down details about Emma, whatever they could find online, in public records and in thorough review of the departmental database. The Yonkers cops stood sentry outside on the porch, securing the scene from anyone who got wind of this on a scanner or the ten o'clock news. Those poor guys went on the air first, but rarely, if ever, did anything become official in the Big Apple until the three big stations, the network owned and operated CBS, NBC and ABC, reported it at eleven o'clock.

Photos were taken of every inch of the small one-bedroom house before Tommy and Maggie started combing it over in a carefully plotted grid system. A clerk at headquarters discovered through online records that Emma Kelly bought the place back in 1974 when she first started with the NYPD. She never moved anywhere. So, any secrets that led her down this deadly path were likely inside these walls or would be buried with her forever. Nor did she list any next of kin on her employment application.

They started in the living room just inside the front door and decided they would work their way back toward the bedroom and kitchen. They didn't know how much time they'd have before the feds and department officials showed up...along with TV crews...so they'd have to make the most of their time in short order.

Tommy canvassed the left side of the room while Maggie went right. Carefully, their gloved hands inspected everything in Emma's world, from the books she read to the knickknacks she saved and there were plenty.

Maggie held a vintage snow globe in her hand from Niagara Falls. She guessed it dated back to the sixties and was probably a souvenir of a happier time.

"Well, lookie here," Tommy called her over to the mantel mélange of assorted photos.

268

Fractured

"Recognize anyone?" He asked Maggie quite matter-of-factly.

She was surprised to see it was a family photo...but not of Emma's family...it was Tiffany Paris' family. Tiffany, her mother and her brother. An unlikely trio in an unlikely place.

A killer's souvenir? Obviously. But which killer?

Clues began dropping into place as their paper bootied feet stepped their way through Emma's life. The blue shoe covers were probably redundant since the hoards had now descended on the scene. Special Agents Quinn and Sutton explained that their boss, Halsey, was staying behind for the press conference while they were there to assist with the investigation.

Quinn and Sutton had no problem eating crow admitting their earlier profile was slightly off but insisted the Binky Killer was definitely a strong male force who was likely not yet aware that Emma was dead.

There had to be at least ten people now inside the compact nine-hundred-square-foot house. There was so much crisscrossing, so much contamination, so many ungloved hands. It was laughable how most crime scenes were handled.

Bedrooms and bathrooms were probably where most people kept their secrets locked away in armoires full of sex toys to medicine cabinets full of opioids. But not Emma's house. Her house was as white and mushy as milk toast but that didn't mean her bedroom and her bathroom didn't contain a Pandora's Box of trouble.

Her pink and grey tiled bathroom was mid-century perfect where everything was tiled including the toothbrush

Lisa Fantino

holder and soap dish mounted to the wall. Tommy saw there was one pink toothbrush lonely in its place next to three empty slots. A pink razor rested in a rubber corner tray suctioned to the shower wall. The room was an orderly corner in an ordinary life.

"Well, well," he said as he looked inside the medicine cabinet. Tommy was talking to himself but ready to reveal all to the others. A man's black toothbrush in a separate caddy with a tube of sensitive toothpaste were tucked inside, hidden in plain sight. He called in forensics to immediately dust all of it for prints and bag and tag it for DNA.

If Emma's man was the Binky Killer, if his prints were in the system, maybe not as a criminal but as a gun owner, or even a cop, they might be able to nail him. At the very least they would compare his prints and DNA to every database on record from criminal to military to Homeland Security. With any luck, they'd catch him this time...and bring him in for questioning. They sent an image of the prints from both toothbrushes into the lab and would have their answer shortly.

A typical single person's kitchen revealed itself to Special Agents Sutton and Quinn who canvassed the yellow room. It was more than buttermilk yellow. It was bright like living inside a giant sunflower decorated with red gingham curtains and roosters. Everything was put away and everything was in its place. The only items in the dish drainboard were a single bowl, single coffee mug and one fork and spoon, all dusted for prints along with the kitchen counters and almost any other tangible surface.

The bulletin board over the old-school wall phone displayed notes and business cards for plumbers and handymen. That was yet another difference between what men

Fractured

and women keep handy. Women know whom to call in an emergency, while men would rather try it themselves.

"Look at this," Sutton showed her partner. "The notes are written by two different people. The handwriting's clearly different."

Target practice, June 27th 1:30p was written on a hot pink postie and stuck to the board with a red pushpin. The curve of the letters, the flourish at the end of words, indicated it was the handwriting of a female, most likely Emma's and someone who was right-handed.

A Best Buy receipt for a new computer was tacked up with a blue pushpin. The receipt showed the buyer's signature as clear as day, *Donovan Kelly*. The writing was a clumsy mix of print and cursive and clearly the slant was that of a leftie. Was this Emma's brother? They'd already been advised she had no next of kin. In fact, the department's personnel records indicated she was unmarried and an only child. So, who was Donovan Kelly and where was he now?

Tommy found Maggie sitting on the edge of the bed holding an old metal lunchbox in her lap. She was staring down, lost in thought as she perused its contents, oblivious to Tommy who called her name twice before she snapped to attention.

The bifold closet doors were wide open. On the right, Tommy saw orderly rows of dowdy women's clothing, neatly pressed floral tops hanging from a top rod and pull-on knit pants and skirts on the bottom. On the left there were dark sweats and hoodies, men's jeans and bulky sweaters. And up at the ceiling, over the closet shelf on the left, was a gaping hole where an acoustic tile had dropped out of its track.

Maggie explained she saw that the tile was pushed back and when she jostled it with a coat hanger, Scooby-Doo dropped like a dead weight, nearly hitting her on the head.

Inside the metal box was everything the Binky Killer had ever taken from any victim both fifteen years ago and most recently. Every ring, trinket, photo, baby tooth, lock of hair, some of which they hoped could lead back to the victims through DNA testing. It would take a while for the samples to be processed but Maggie and Tommy were almost certain they had just nabbed not one but two killers. Two nuts from the same family tree? It was looking that way.

"What's that?" Tommy questioned his partner about the document lying next to her on the bed. It looked official and made him wonder.

"Oh, yeah, icing on the cake," she said, lifting Emma's birth certificate up to Tommy for inspection.

"Turns out Emma's Daddy Dearest was Richard McNamara…no religious title indicated on the birth certificate here, but the man listed as her father had the same birthday as our first dead padre.

"I always say there's no such thing as coincidence except in the dictionary."

"This just gets better and better," Tommy said in utter awe of the crime scene before him and the secrets it revealed.

Chapter Seventy

What they found was shocking. A double life, a troubled soul, two lives with one purpose.

Friday night led into Saturday morning as investigators tried to make sense of it all. But how do you make sense out of madness? An exercise like that is the very definition of insanity.

CSU had reported back with a quick analysis of the fingerprints from the bathroom, the man's toothbrush, Emma's hairbrush, the Scooby-Doo lunchbox and all its treasures, the pink postie and the Best Buy receipt. They all belonged to Emma Kelly, every bit of trace evidence, every death scene souvenir, every man's razor and every woman's sweater in the closet, tucked away with all of her secrets. There wasn't another set of fingerprints in the entire house. She was all alone, after all.

It would take a bit longer, a few days even with a rush, to get the DNA results but the team knew in their gut they had nabbed both killers. Emma and Donovan. Not husband and wife. Not brother and sister. But one in the same.

Mental disease and defect can lurk in the corner of a troubled mind for years before breaking free and once unleashed there's no putting it back in the bottle. It's a kink in a biological web of neurons that troubles even those trained to deal with it.

"It's hard to admit we missed the signs of dissociative identity disorder," said Special Agent Quinn. It was uniquely hard for him since the darkness of the mind was his specialty.

It was four in the morning as Quinn and Special Agent Sutton sat with Maggie and Tommy, Lopez and Summers, draped in their government-issued chairs. Hard on their backs but providing the only support for their weary bodies at this late hour. The brass, both local and feds, had gone home long ago.

"A fractured mind shatters in childhood and manifests itself in adulthood," Quinn lectured the group.

"It goes back to that love map doesn't it?" Summers asked. His acerbic wit was not lost on the group despite their extreme fatigue.

"It does," Quinn confirmed with as much of a smile as he could muster, pushed down by exhaustion and defeat. "If her father was a priest and her mother was a hooker, who knows what she experienced as a child. Psychological abuse or emotional neglect is just as destructive as physical abuse and it's more common than you think."

He explained that adult stress can often crack the veneer of the main personality, forcing others to the surface to cope with a change in life or circumstances that's just too hard to bear.

"9/11 rocked this city to its core. It literally destroyed the very foundation of many lives." Sutton didn't need to remind the people in that room. The nation watched the tragedy of that day unfold on TV but New Yorkers lived through it, second by second, day by day, literally inhaling the toxic dust for months. There were no words, just emptiness, shock and fear.

Fractured

"Emma Kelly, like so many, had no one and no place to turn," Quinn tried to explain to the group what he himself didn't understand. "It was like she was thrown into a war with no coping skills and only one of her personalities could win.

"Everyday she arrived in lower Manhattan, walking through an ash cloud of yesterday, not sure whether tomorrow would even come.

"It was post-traumatic stress disorder magnified with infinite repercussions for someone like Emma."

He explained that Donovan was most likely born out of Emma's insecurity. Donovan could've been there since a neglected childhood but he manifested when he was needed to deal with life's harsh realities.

"Emma needed to take control of her life and eliminate any perceived weakness," Quinn continued. "Once she was promoted and she had settled into her new position, there was no need for Donovan until retirement pulled the rug out from under Emma and the cycle began again."

And their cycle of crime would begin again for each of them in just a few hours. A new shift, the next homicide, more of the same but different. Any misconception of a normal day on the job had been shattered forever.

Epilogue

Maggie could hear the boom and pop of fireworks in the distance as she headed up the West Side Highway. Tommy and Helen had invited her to a Fourth of July barbecue but she needed a quiet night with Uncle Bobby to sip a glass of merlot and savor every twirl of *pasta con le sarde*, spaghetti with fennel leaves, roasted pine nuts, raisins and sardines.

In six short weeks, in the short span between summer holidays, Maggie had come to realize how lucky she was to reach this point in life with her love map intact.

She sat with Uncle Bobby watching the fireworks from every corner of his riverfront balcony. They sat in silence as the noise exploded around them, both knowing the importance of having at least one person in your corner of this crazy world can make all the difference.

The loose ends from his biggest case had been tied up by the young detective he loved like a daughter. There were no words as they watched the night sky light up, just a shared comfortable exhaustion between them.

Fractured

As Maggie returned home, she reached into the front pocket of her purse for the keys and fumbled in the darkness with something which caught her by surprise. She had forgotten to remove Nonna's rosary beads after the failed sting at Saint Anthony's.

As her head hit the downy pillow that night, she prayed...for the first time in a long time. To a mother she never knew. For a father who made her strong. And for the strength to continue doing the work she was born to do.

About the Author

Lisa Fantino is an award-winning journalist and attorney whose best-selling travel memoir, "Amalfi Blue - lost & found in the south of Italy," has been Number One in the U.S., Canada and Australia and Top Ten on three continents.

As a broadcaster she spent a career on the air at New York's top news stations, WCBS-AM and WINS-AM, and as an anchor at the NBC Radio Networks. As an attorney she has represented clients in both state and federal courts.

Lisa's passion for reading and storytelling is in her DNA. While her Dad taught her a great love of reading, her Mom created stories so she wouldn't have to read. It was the best of both worlds for a budding author.

With "Fractured," her third book, she introduces gutsy rookie Detective Maggie Flynn with a New York street edge seasoned with just enough Italian to make life passionate.

Visit her website:
AuthorLisaFantino.com

Made in the USA
Columbia, SC
19 June 2019